"Dance with me," Justin said when another ballad came on.

Siobhan followed him back out to the dance floor and wrapped her arms around his neck.

"I'm glad they're playing a lot of slow songs, because I like holding you in my arms."

"I like it, too."

A slow grin curved Justin's lips. "Then we'll need to do it more often." He touched his mouth to hers.

"Every chance we get," he whispered.

They danced through every slow song that played, and by the time he took her home, her body and mind were in a jumble.

"Thank you, again, for coming to the party with me," she said as they stood in her entryway.

"I enjoyed myself."

She leaned up, intending to give him a quick kiss, but as soon as their lips touched and he swept his hot tongue into her mouth, all rational thoughts went out the window. Justin deepened the kiss, thoroughly exploring every inch of her mouth.

He broke it off and rested his forehead against hers. "I'd better leave while I still can."

Siobhan nodded, though she wasn't sure she really wanted him to leave. He kissed her once more and slipped out the door.

She closed her eyes and leaned against it, her breathing still ragged. She hadn't planned on meeting a man like him and didn't know how long she would be able to keep her guard up.

Dear Reader,

I'm excited to introduce you to The Grays of Los Angeles. Nolan and DeAnna Gray have worked hard to build a legacy for their children. But their most fervent desire is for each of them to experience the joy of an enduring love.

First is Siobhan Gray, the oldest of five, dynamic PR director and a certified control freak. *Spontaneous* isn't in her vocabulary...until she meets Justin Cartwright. Justin is just the man to show her how to have a little fun because, frankly, he's forgotten, too. I thoroughly enjoyed watching them learn to balance work, fun and falling in love. I hope you do, as well.

I appreciate your emails and messages. I love hearing from you!

Baby sister Morgan Gray takes center stage next, and I can't wait for you to see what's in store for her. Fast cars, football and, just maybe, love.

Much love,

Sheryl

Website: SherylLister.com
Email: sheryllister@gmail.com
Facebook: Author Sheryl Lister

Tender Kisses

SHERYL LISTER

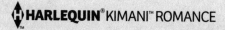

HARLEQUIN® KIMANI™ ROMANCE

Recycling programs
for this product may
not exist in your area.

ISBN-13: 978-0-373-86447-8

Tender Kisses

H HARLEQUIN®
™ www.Harlequin.com

Printed in U.S.A.

Sheryl Lister has enjoyed reading and writing for as long as she can remember. She writes contemporary and inspirational romance and romantic suspense. Her first novel, *Just to Be with You*, earned her a 2015 Romance Slam Jam nomination for Debut Author of the Year. When she's not reading, writing or playing chauffeur, Sheryl can be found on a date with her husband or in the kitchen creating appetizers and bite-size desserts. Sheryl resides in California and is a wife and a mother of three daughters and a son-in-love. She's also a grandmother to a very special little boy.

Books by Sheryl Lister

Harlequin Kimani Romance

Visit the Author Profile page at
Harlequin.com for more titles.

To my husband, Lance, my children, family and friends
for your continued support. I appreciate and love you!

Acknowledgments

My Heavenly Father, thank You for my life.

A special thank you to the readers and authors
I've met on this journey. You've enriched my life
in more ways than you know.

Special thank you to my editor, Rachel Burkot,
for your editorial guidance and support. I'll miss you!

A very special thank you to my agent, Sarah E. Younger.
I appreciate you more than words can say.

Chapter 1

I wonder if I can hold my breath for five minutes. Siobhan Gray tried to edge away and create some space between her and her dance partner. The potency of the man's cologne—she swore he had bathed in it—had her on the verge of passing out. Instead of holding her breath, maybe she should take one big whiff and put herself out of this misery. The effect would be the same.

"You seem too young to be handling all the PR for your family's company," he said, breaking into her thoughts.

She pasted a smile on her face while he went on and on about Gray Home Safety. She caught the gazes of her two best friends, who stood across the room with wide grins. Siobhan rolled her eyes and groaned inwardly.

"Did you say something?" her dance partner asked.

Had that groan slipped out? "No, nothing. Just humming along with the music," she lied. *How long is this song, anyway?* When it finally ended, he didn't release her.

"Isn't this nice?" he asked, tightening his hold.

About as nice as dancing naked in an ice storm. The move came with another gust of his cologne, and Siobhan nearly gagged. She was done. "If you'll excuse me, there's someone I need to speak to." She stepped away from him so fast she stumbled, but quickly righted herself.

He caught her arm. "Are you okay?"

She gave him a tense smile. "Fine, thanks. And thank you for the dance." She turned and started from the floor. Three steps in, she realized he was right behind her.

"Hold on a minute." He chuckled nervously. "I was hoping, Sio—Siyo—"

"Sha-von," she said impatiently.

"Yes, yes. It's a nice name. What I wanted to ask, *Siobhan,* is do you think you can pass along my card to your father? I have this great home—"

Siobhan cut him off and ignored the business card in his hand. "Mr...."

"Benson," he supplied.

"Mr. Benson, if you have a product, idea or anything else, you should speak directly to my father or my brother Brandon." She pointed them out. "Now, if you'll excuse me." She stalked off without waiting for his reply and headed straight for the balcony.

Once outside, she inhaled deeply and drew in a lungful of the sweet night air. She braced her hands on the railing and tried to rein in her anger. As PR director for Gray Home Safety, it seemed as if every man in attendance at tonight's gala thought they could sweet-talk their way into the family's company. Siobhan had been here for only an hour and, so far, four men had approached her. The conversations started pleasantly enough but, within a few minutes, ended the same—with a pitch for the next great thing in home safety. She had heard it all, from stair lifts to heated shower chairs.

She was proud of the company her father had started upon his discharge from the army. While he had returned whole, his best friend had not. Disheartened by the difficulty in getting services and accommodations for the disabled, Nolan Gray decided to do something about it by designing them himself. Her father's friend, Thaddeus Whitcomb, joined the company as a minor partner soon after. More than two decades later, the small company housed in their garage was now one of the largest in-home safety companies in the country. Her brother Khalil had taken the company to a new level when he designed accessible equipment for the fitness center he opened two years ago.

"Here you are, Siobhan. We wondered where you went."

Siobhan turned from the rail to find her two best friends. "I bet you did, Cynthia."

"We saw you dancing. Was he a nice man?" Cynthia Johnson was a die-hard romantic. From the time the three of them became best friends in fourth grade, Cynthia had been planning their happily-ever-afters. Siobhan was the only one who hadn't found her prince.

"Of course he wasn't," Kendra Martin tossed out with a chuckle. "Didn't you see her face, Cyn?"

"It couldn't have been that bad."

Kendra leaned close to Siobhan and wrinkled her nose. "Girl, what kind of perfume is that?"

"I'm not wearing any perfume. It must be what's left of Mr. Benson's cologne. I thought I was going to pass out."

Kendra waved a hand. "That is not cologne. It smells more like toi—"

"Don't say it," Cynthia interrupted.

The three women looked at each other and burst out laughing. Siobhan shook her head. "He was the worst of the four men tonight." She frowned. "I'm tired of men trying to come on to me for the sole purpose of working their way into the family business." She had already traveled that road and had the remnants of the broken heart to prove it.

And she was still trying to rebuild her bank account from the fiasco.

"Well, if you dressed like you were thirty-three, instead of seventy-three, men would be tossing you something more than their business cards," Kendra said bluntly.

Siobhan stared down at her dress. "What's wrong with my dress?"

"I think it's beautiful," Cynthia said.

Kendra rolled her eyes. "It is a beautiful dress...for my *grandmother*. For one thing, it's long sleeved. For another, you're all buttoned up like a nun. It's all right to show a little cleavage. And, to be honest, it's too big."

Siobhan placed her hand on her hip. "Why don't you tell me how you really feel, Kendra? I'm not wearing some dress so tight I can barely walk."

"It doesn't have to be skintight, but the material should at least do a drive-by on your curves."

"In case you've forgotten, I'm a size fourteen, not four."

"And with your five-eight height, those curves are in all the right places. Hell, if I had any semblance of your shape, you'd better believe I'd be flaunting it."

"I don't do this often," Cynthia started, "but I have to agree with Kendra this time."

Siobhan sighed heavily. She knew her body was in good shape, toned and tight in all the right places, but had dressed purposely to keep men at a distance.

"Stop letting Arthur ruin your life," Cynthia added softly.

Siobhan turned back to the rail, not wanting them to see how much Arthur's deception still affected her. After two years, the mention of his name shouldn't conjure up all the same hurt and anger, but it did.

Kendra came and stood next to her. "Siobhan, you have so much going for you. You're intelligent, beautiful and one of the sweetest people I know. Stop hiding. It's time for you to come out and play again. You were always the outgoing, fun one when we were growing up. Ever since—"

"I'm *fine*, Kendra. That was a long time ago, and I'm over it." Siobhan's two friends viewed her skeptically. "I'm still the same me—fun and outgoing. I just haven't found anyone to have fun with," she added wryly, trying to lighten the mood. Though truthfully, she hadn't been looking for fun. All she wanted was to do her job and make her family proud.

Cynthia, standing on the other side of Siobhan, playfully bumped Siobhan's shoulder. "You never know—your real Prince Charming could be here tonight and you're out here sulking."

"I don't know what I'm going to do with you two," Siobhan muttered.

Kendra laughed. "Hey, we're trying to get a couple of godchildren. Cyn's baby girl and this one here," she said, rubbing her baby bump, "need a godsister or brother."

Siobhan glanced down and smiled. "Somehow, I think I may have to settle for being a godmother." She was thirty-three years old and, as much as she wanted marriage and children, Siobhan didn't see herself allowing another man to get close. In fact, she thought it better to officially retire from the game of love altogether.

"Thanks for the invite." Justin Cartwright shook his longtime friend's hand. He and Robert Mitchell had been college roommates and bonded through their mutual love of technology. While Justin had continued to pursue a career in technology, Bobby changed directions to help his ailing grandfather run the family's winery.

"No problem, man. I figured with all the home-safety companies here tonight, you could get that next idea off the ground. It's even better than the first one. I can't tell you how much I love your first one. Those electronic floor sensors are the best I've seen on the market. If this next one is as good, you'll have companies lined up."

"I appreciate the endorsement, Bobby. Maybe I should have you taking care of marketing," he added with a chuckle.

"Five years ago, I might've taken you up on your offer. Now I actually like the wine business." Bobby's gaze shifted to a man approaching then back to Justin. "That's Charles Hickson. He might be someone you want to talk to." Bobby had contacts throughout the business world.

Justin nodded and greeted the man in question. He had read up on Hickson's company, as well as several others. But he was interested in only one company—Gray Home Safety, one of the largest in the country. The floor sensors had done well and afforded him a comfortable lifestyle, but partnering with the Grays would catapult Justin's new idea to another level and have far-reaching benefits for both parties. He'd researched everything he could find on the company and determined working with them would be his best shot at making his new alert system a household name. "What do you know about Gray Home Safety?"

"The Grays?"

"Yeah. You know them?"

"We met about a year ago. They're cool people, down-to-earth. At least a couple of his sons and daughters work there. The one brother I met is a sharp businessman. The daughter is a helluva PR director. I've never seen anybody handle the media and negative press the way she does. On the personal side, she's pretty nice but tends to keep people at a distance. Is that the company you're targeting?"

"Yes. I want the best, and they're it."

Bobby smiled. "I can introduce you, if you want."

"No, thanks. I'm sure I can handle an introduction." Justin scanned the ballroom again and zeroed in on the beautiful woman on the dance floor. He had spotted her when she arrived earlier and noticed that she carried herself with the regal bearing of a queen. She was tall, wore her hair in a short curly style and had him absolutely mesmerized. He hadn't been able to keep his concentration on the task at hand for staring at her. His gaze narrowed. That was the third or fourth man he had seen her dancing with. Either she was very popular, or she was somebody big in the safety industry. The latter didn't bother him because he had only one company in mind. He kept one eye on her while sipping his drink and listening to Bobby. When the song ended, Justin watched as the man followed the woman from the dance floor and handed her what appeared to be a business card. Just as he suspected, the man was trying to pitch his idea. "Excuse me, Bobby. I want to do some mingling. I'll catch up with you later."

Bobby nodded. "Good luck. Not that you need it. Let me know if there's anything I can do. I'm cutting out early. So, I'll call you later this week."

The two men parted ways, and Justin headed in the direction he saw her go. Halfway there, a man caught his arm.

"Well, if it isn't Justin Cartwright. How've you been?" he said, grabbing Justin's hand.

The man pumped Justin's arm so hard he thought it would fall off. "Just fine, sir."

He grinned. "I've been keeping up with you and hearing some great things about your sensors."

"Really?" Three years ago, Justin had approached the man about backing his floor sensors and had been all but tossed out of the office. But he had persevered without any backing, and now his floor sensors were among the best available.

"Yes, yes. So, do you have any new products coming to market?"

"Not yet. If you'll excuse me, I need to speak to someone. Enjoy your evening." Not waiting for a reply, he left the man standing there. As much as he wanted to tell the man exactly where he could go, Justin didn't believe in burning bridges in business. Now it was back to his original mission—the beauty in gold. For a moment, he lost her in the crowd then spotted her exiting to the balcony

on the far side of the room. Two other people stopped him
before he made it to the balcony.

"If I have to dance with one more scheming stuffed
shirt, I swear I'm going to give him a swift kick in the shin
with the pointed toe of this shoe. I bet he'll think twice…"
he heard her say as he reached the open door.

Justin went still. He took two steps back, pivoted and
headed for the bar. *Damn!* He had to rethink his strategy.
He ordered a Coke, not wanting anything to cloud his
thinking. He took the drink out to the opposite balcony
and leaned against the rail.

"Now what?" he muttered. Truth be told, he shouldn't
be worried about a woman. He had more pressing things on
his plate, like making sure his alert system was perfected
and talking with Mr. Gray tonight. He sipped his drink
and stared at the grounds below. A slow smile curved his
mouth as an idea came to him. He was great at multitask-
ing and wanted only a dance. There would be plenty of
time to get that pitch in. Justin downed the remainder of
his drink and went back inside.

He greeted and made small talk with several people, all
while maneuvering closer to the woman. "Good evening,
ladies." She stood talking with two other women, and seeing her from a distance had not come close to capturing
her beauty, especially her eyes. They were a lighter shade
of brown and perfectly complemented her golden-brown
skin. Soft laughter from one of the women made him realize he was staring like an awestruck teen. Justin quickly
gathered himself and stuck out his hand to the first woman,
who was still smiling. "I'm Justin Cartwright."

"Kendra Martin. Nice to meet you, Justin."

"I'm Cynthia Johnson," the second woman said, extending her hand.

"Nice to meet you both." He turned slightly to face the
woman he had been studying all night. "And you are?"

"Siobhan. Siobhan Hunter," she said, shaking his outstretched hand.

"It's a pleasure to meet you, Siobhan," Justin said, his eyes never leaving hers. The warmth flowing from her touch gave him pause. The slight widening of her eyes and the way she pulled back let him know he wasn't the only one who felt it. "Are you ladies enjoying yourselves?"

"Yes," Siobhan and Cynthia chorused.

Kendra angled her head. "Let's say the night just got more interesting."

Justin lifted a brow. "Is that right?"

"Definitely." She hooked her arm with the other woman and led her away. "Come on, Cynthia. We should probably go find our husbands. You know how they get. Nice to meet you, Justin," she called over her shoulder. "Chat with you later, Siobhan."

He chuckled. "She's real subtle, isn't she?"

"You'll have to excuse Kendra."

"No harm done. Since she left us all alone, I say we take advantage of it. I wouldn't want her efforts to go to waste."

Siobhan smiled and said softly, "I guess not."

"Would you like to dance?"

She hesitated briefly then placed her soft hand in his.

Justin led her out to the dance floor, slid his arm around her waist and pulled her close to his body, but was careful enough to leave a respectable space between them. He didn't want to scare her off, or potentially feel the pointed toe of her shoe in his shin before he had a chance to finish the dance. "So, are you with one of the safety companies?" She turned her face to meet his eyes. In her heels, she stood only a couple of inches shorter than his six-one height.

She stiffened in his embrace. "Yes. Why?"

"I assume since this is a safety awards gala that everyone here is either affiliated with a company or looking to do so. And I was wondering if you enjoyed your job."

"Let me guess. You have the next greatest safety invention you want to pitch," she said almost accusingly.

Remembering the look on her face when the last man handed her his card, he said, "Actually, I just want to dance with you. Have we met before? You seem familiar—"

Siobhan viewed him skeptically. "Really?" She stepped out of his arms, held out her hand and said curtly, "How about we skip to the part where you hand me your business card and stop wasting my time?"

A no-nonsense sister. Justin reclaimed the distance and pulled her back into his embrace. "I don't have a business card to give you." Well, that wasn't exactly true. He had several in his breast pocket, but, since he had finagled an invite to this shindig only to meet someone from Gray Home Safety, which she wasn't part of, he didn't want to pull one out and ruin his chances.

She stared at him for several seconds then relaxed in his arms. "So, Justin, are you in the home-safety business?"

"I have a couple of products on the market," he answered carefully. He felt her body stiffen again and added quickly, "And I like working for myself." They continued swaying to the slow jazz tune without conversing. Someone bumped Siobhan, pushing her closer to him, and he groaned inwardly. Her voluptuous body molded to his, and it took every inch of his control not to take advantage. His hands wanted nothing more than to tour each curve and conduct his own private touch test.

Easing back a fraction, Justin hit the brakes on his runaway thoughts. He needed to remember the plan—a dance, then find Mr. Gray. And that plan didn't include fantasies of exploring a more personal relationship with Siobhan Hunter.

Now, if he could just get his body to go along…

Chapter 2

Siobhan didn't want to be affected by the handsome man she danced with. But every time she tried to put some space between them, someone on the crowded dance floor bumped her, forcing their bodies closer together. Unlike her previous dance partner's offensive cologne, Justin's scent was more like an aphrodisiac. She had a hard time not staring at his clean-shaven mahogany-brown face with eyes to match, and he had a deep baritone voice that made her body tingle in places long forgotten. Places she had purposely closed off. Justin Cartwright. He said she seemed familiar, and she searched her memory banks, but couldn't recall ever hearing his name. Then again, there was no way she would forget a man like him.

While dancing, she attempted to figure out his angle. Sure, he said he wanted only to dance, but so did the other half-dozen men who approached her tonight, then changed their tune as soon as, or not long after, the song ended, which was why she had given him her mother's maiden name instead of her family name.

"You never answered my question."

Siobhan's brows knit in confusion. "I'm sorry—what did you ask?"

Justin chuckled. "I asked how you liked your job, but we got a little sidetracked when you nearly ripped my head off."

"Sorry about that," she said contritely. "I love a challenge and my job provides that."

"Sounds intriguing, but don't the challenges become a hassle day in and day out?"

"Every day isn't like that. Most times my day is stacked with meetings, working on press releases and fielding phone calls. And, as the oldest of five, putting out fires is second nature," she added wryly.

"I can imagine."

"Do you have any siblings?"

"Two younger sisters. Something we have in common— being the oldest…and putting out fires."

Siobhan laughed.

"Maybe we can swap stories over coffee or dinner."

Her laughter faded. "Um, I don't have time to date."

"Why not? You're a beautiful woman. I'm sure there are men lined up waiting to take you out."

She laughed him off. But in reality, over the past two years, the only men who seemed remotely interested in her had ulterior motives. "I think the song is over." Actually, they had danced through at least three. "Thank you for the dance, Justin." She turned to walk away, and he caught her hand.

"May I buy you a drink?"

"No, thank you. Have a good evening." She wove her way through the crowd of people who flooded the dance floor in response to the sounds of a popular tune now playing. Siobhan exited the ballroom and ducked into the nearest bathroom. Her heart raced, and her hands shook.

She stared at her reflection in the mirror. Obviously, the loose-fitting dress she had deliberately chosen to keep men at bay hadn't deterred Justin. All while they danced, his gaze never left hers. At one point, he stared at her as if she were his favorite dessert, and for a moment, she allowed the thought to play around in her mind. Heat rose in her cheeks, and she fanned herself in an effort to cool off. Where in the world had that thought come from? Siobhan smoothed down the front of her gown, took a deep breath and left the bathroom. Rounding the corner, she hit a solid mass. Strong arms steadied her.

"Are you okay, Siobhan?" Justin asked, still holding her.

"Yes. Fine. Sorry—I wasn't watching where I was going. Thanks for the save. I need to speak to my friends before they leave."

"You're welcome. I'll walk you over."

"Huh? Oh, you don't need to do that. I'm sure there are some other people who you probably want to talk to about your products."

A lazy grin curved his mouth. "Are you trying to get rid of me?"

Yes! "No, nothing like that. I—"

"Glad to hear it." He extended his arm.

Sighing inwardly, Siobhan hooked her arm in his and let him escort her back to the ballroom and over to her two friends and their husbands. She made introductions, and the men struck up a conversation.

Kendra pulled Siobhan to the side. "Girl, you'd better snap up all that fine dark chocolate before some other woman does."

Cynthia giggled and nodded her head enthusiastically. "I agree. You two looked so good dancing together."

"I see some gorgeous godchildren in my future," Kendra added.

Siobhan snapped her head around. "Wait—what? Hold

up a minute. Nobody's having anybody's babies," she whispered tersely.

"Siobhan?" Justin touched her arm.

Glaring at Kendra once more, she turned. "Yes, Justin," she said pleasantly.

"I need to talk to someone real quick. Will you save me one more dance?"

As much as she wanted to tell him no, with everyone staring at her, she couldn't. "Sure."

He clasped her hand and gave it a gentle squeeze. "Thank you."

His heated gaze caused Siobhan's breath to stall in her lungs. He smiled then sauntered off with the sexiest walk she had ever seen on a man. She didn't realize she had been holding her breath until Cynthia's voice broke through her thoughts.

"Girl," she said slowly, "do not let that man get away. I don't care if he's pitching an idea or not."

"Amen, sister. *Amen*," Kendra said, shaking her head. "He looks like a man who could curl your toes in the bedroom."

Siobhan's gaze followed Justin until he disappeared in the crowd. She could still feel the tingling in her palm and rubbed her other hand over the spot, hoping to erase the feeling. "The only thing he's getting is that one dance. Nothing more."

True to his word, Justin returned a while later for the dance. Siobhan steeled herself against the unwanted sensations that coursed through her when he wrapped his arm around her waist and moved his body close to hers. She silently prayed for the song to end, although this time for a different reason. Everything about this man turned her on, and she didn't want to be *turned on*. Before the last note faded away, she backed out of his arms. "I think I'm going to call it a night. It was very nice to meet you, Justin."

"I'll walk you out." Without waiting for her response, Justin entwined their fingers and led her out and toward the front of the hotel. "Did you valet park?"

"Yes." She tried to disengage their hands, but he tightened his grip and kept walking. "Justin, you really don't have to walk me out."

A sexy grin tipped the corners of Justin's mouth. "If I don't walk you out, I can't persuade you to meet me for coffee tomorrow."

"I told you already that I'm busy and don't have time to date."

"True, but I'm not asking you out on a date. Think of it as two people with a similar past hanging out and sharing stories. Do you have your ticket?" he asked as they pushed through the front door.

He released her hand. Siobhan reached in her purse for the ticket and handed it to the valet.

"Do you live in the area?"

"Not too far away. Why?"

Justin pulled a card and pen from his pocket, wrote something on the back and handed it to her. "This is the address of a nearby coffee shop. Since you're local, it shouldn't be too far for you. I'd love it if you met me there tomorrow morning. Is eleven a good time?"

She stared at the card for several seconds then took it. "No promises."

"Ma'am, your car," the valet said.

"Thank you." Facing Justin, she said, "Good night."

"Good night, Siobhan. I've enjoyed your company tonight."

He squeezed her hand again, this time rubbing his thumb in small circles on her palm. She almost melted in a heap on the concrete. She hurried around to the driver's side of her car and slid in behind the wheel. She could still see him standing there as she pulled off. There was no way she planned to be at that coffee shop in the morning. Justin Cartwright was a temptation she couldn't afford.

Justin waited until the taillights of Siobhan's Lexus SUV disappeared before going back inside. He searched the ballroom for Mr. Gray or his partner Mr. Whitcomb but didn't see either man. Making some discreet inquiries, he located both men standing in a group. As soon as there was a break in the conversation and the small gathering dispersed, Justin headed over.

"Good evening, Mr. Gray." Justin extended his hand.

Mr. Gray shook Justin's hand. "Good evening, young man. Have we met?"

"No, sir. My name is Justin Cartwright, and I was hoping to talk to you about an in-home alert system I'm working on."

"Well, I'm always looking for something new and exciting, but aren't there a couple on the market already?"

"Yes, but neither of those systems are able to sense body temperature, and mine can." Well, it would when he could figure out how to make it work properly. He was still having some trouble with it distinguishing from the room temperature.

Mr. Gray's eyebrow lifted a fraction. "Is that right?" He reached into his breast pocket, pulled out a card and handed it to Justin. "Why don't you call my secretary next week and she'll put you on my calendar. I'm looking forward to hearing about this system."

Justin accepted the card. "Thank you, sir. I'm looking forward to it, as well. I won't take up any more of your time. Have a good evening." He waited until Mr. Gray walked away before going in the other direction. On the outside, Justin maintained a cool facade, but inside he was cheering.

Since there was no one else he wanted to talk to, Justin kept going until he reached the exit. He thought about Siobhan. With any luck, she would be at the coffee shop in the morning.

* * *

Lying in bed later, Justin's mind drifted back to Siobhan—her eyes, incredible lips and generous curves. He was especially captivated by her directness. It probably warned most men off, but had the exact opposite effect on him. A woman hadn't caught his attention in a while, but the no-nonsense businesswoman had made a deep impression upon him.

The last long-term relationship he had been in ended a year ago. He had been content with the date nights, good sex and casual conversation, but his ex wanted more than he was prepared to give—marriage and a family—so they parted ways. His focus had been solely on making his product the best on the market, especially after his grandfather died in a home accident that could have been prevented had someone found him sooner.

Justin felt partially responsible because he hadn't been as focused on his work and put the alert system he was designing on the back burner. He had dated multiple women since then, but none lasted beyond a few dates. He was careful not to give any woman the notion he wanted anything permanent. Maybe he would be ready to settle down in a few years. For now, he had one goal: partnering with Gray Home Safety and making sure no one else suffered the same loss.

By morning, he lay awake in bed still thinking about Siobhan and wondering whether she would show up at the coffee shop later. Justin tossed the covers back, dressed and went out for his morning run. He tried to get in at least three miles four times a week. The run helped clear his thoughts and gave him the opportunity to sort out, in his mind, any kinks in whatever program he was working on. This morning, however, Siobhan Gray crowded the space in his brain. He started with a slow jog until he reached the nearby park trail then increased his pace.

One of the things he liked about living in LA was the weather. The cloudless, early-spring morning was warm enough that he didn't need to wear a jacket. His feet pounded the paved trail in a steady rhythm as he mentally went over the changes he wanted to make in his program to track movement in the home. He was having trouble with one of the sensors and couldn't figure out why it stopped working after a certain amount of time. Since he renewed his focus on the project nine months ago, Justin had seen similar products hit the market, but he'd worked to make sure his had an added feature not available on the current models.

Clearing the shaded area, he slowed to a jog and cut across the park back toward his house. Once there, he grabbed a bottle of water from the refrigerator, downed the contents and went upstairs to shower. He wanted to get to the shop a few minutes before eleven.

His cell rang as he was leaving.

"What's up, Justin?" Bobby said when Justin answered.

"Hey."

"I wanted to find out if you had a chance to talk to Mr. Gray about your project."

"No. We didn't get a chance to discuss it."

"Oh. I thought for sure you'd have it locked up by now. What happened?"

"I only had a chance to introduce myself." He decided not to tell his friend that he had got sidetracked.

"I know I have his number somewhere. I can call and set up a meeting if you want."

"No, that's okay," Justin said hastily. "Mr. Gray gave me his card, and I plan to call first thing tomorrow morning." The last thing he needed was Bobby's interference. His friend meant well, but Justin wanted to do this on his own. "I'm on my way out, so I gotta go."

"All right. I have to fly up to the Bay Area to check on the winery and my grandfather. I'll probably be gone for about six weeks. Let me know if you change your mind."

"Don't worry about me. You know I have no problems

going after what I want. Just save me a bottle of your best wine for the celebration."

"Will do. Later."

He disconnected and pocketed the phone. Hopefully, he would have something to celebrate by the time Bobby returned.

Justin arrived ten minutes before the hour and snagged a table that gave him a good view of the door. He told the server he was waiting for someone and trained his eyes on the entrance. *Five after eleven and no sign of Siobhan.*

Had he overplayed his hand? He thought for sure, with the chemistry brewing between them, she would show up. He drummed his fingers on the table and took another glance at his watch. The server came back to the table and told him he couldn't hold up a table without ordering. "Ten minutes," he told her.

Disappointment filled him when she hadn't arrived by eleven fifteen. He hadn't realized how much he wanted to see her again. Dropping his head in his hands, he contemplated his next move. Whatever the case, he had to vacate the booth. When he arrived he had been starving, but his appetite had waned considerably. Justin slid out of the booth and came to his feet. He took one step and froze. Siobhan came through the door and searched until their gazes locked. His heart rate accelerated, and he smiled. Somehow his excitement went well beyond a casual encounter. His gaze lingered on her face then slowly drifted down. Unlike the loose-fitting gown she wore the previous night, today she had on a short-sleeved fitted T and jeans that hugged her curves. A rush of desire hit him hard and fast.

Siobhan hurried over. "I'm so sorry I'm late. I was talking to my sister and lost track of time."

He bent slightly to kiss her cheek. "No, no. It's all right. I'm just glad you came." He gestured for her to sit and slid back in across from her. "I didn't think you would."

Looking him directly in the eye, she said, "I hadn't planned to. I decided at the last minute."

He had never met a woman so straightforward and who had no problems expressing her opinions. "What made you change your mind?"

She angled her head. "Truthfully, I don't know," she said.

The hesitancy he heard in her voice was a stark contrast to the confidence in her earlier statement. He reached for her hand. "Like I said, I'm glad you came."

The server approached. "I guess you were waiting for someone after all," she mumbled. "What can I get you?" she asked Siobhan.

"A cup of chamomile tea with honey, please."

"And you, sir?"

"Coffee and wheat toast, please." He glanced over at Siobhan when the young lady walked away. "You sure you don't want anything to eat, Siobhan?"

"No. The tea is fine. We're having Sunday dinner at my parents' house this afternoon, and my mom always cooks a feast."

"Do you eat at your parents' house every week?"

"No, but we usually get together about once every month or so. My mom is big on family."

"So is mine, but since my parents live outside of Las Vegas, they're not as easy to visit."

She propped her head on her hands and smiled. "Vegas, huh? I haven't been there in a long while. Need to go again sometime soon."

Her eyes sparkled, and those beautiful gloss-slicked lips curved into a sexy smile. His first thought was booking a flight for two to Las Vegas as soon as he got home.

He was in trouble. *Big* trouble.

Chapter 3

Despite her calm demeanor, Siobhan's stomach was in knots. True, her mother would prepare a feast, but she had ordered the tea because she didn't think anything else would stay down. She had no problems standing in front of the media giving a press conference and had stared down her fiercest competitors. But sitting here with Justin, she felt out of her element. It had taken her until an hour ago to make up her mind to meet him today. Partly because she was curious about his background, and partly because she just wanted to see him again.

The server set a cup of tea and a plate with honey and lemon in front of her, then coffee and toast in front of Justin.

"Usually, men eat more than toast and coffee," Siobhan said after the server departed.

"You're right, but I went for a run earlier and my appetite hasn't quite returned yet."

When they had danced the night before, she'd felt his

hard body against hers. The cut of his expensive suit had done nothing to disguise his muscular build. Today he wore a black T-shirt that fit nicely against his well-defined chest, and she was having a hard time keeping her eyes off his bulging biceps that flexed with every movement as he spread jelly on his toast.

Justin chuckled. "Believe me, in a couple of hours, I'll be hungry enough to eat a horse."

She laughed. "You remind me of my brothers."

"Speaking of brothers, you mentioned being the oldest of five."

"Yes. I have three brothers and one sister."

"Do they all live in the city?"

Siobhan added honey and lemon to her tea then took a sip. She nodded. "Yes. My brother Brandon is one year younger than me, but sometimes acts like he's the oldest. My brother Khalil is three years younger, and the twins, Malcolm and Morgan, six years."

"Wow, you have a big family."

"What about your family? You mentioned having two sisters."

He finished chewing before speaking. "There's a nine-year age difference between me and my sister Yvonne, and thirteen between me and Jocelyn. Yvonne is a forensic scientist, and Jocelyn is a junior in college majoring in electrical engineering."

"Wow. That's a huge age gap."

"Tell me about it," he said, shaking his head. "I wasn't too happy about having to share my parents after such a long time, but I love my sisters more than anything *now…* though they drove me absolutely crazy when they were little."

Siobhan laughed. "I can imagine. My brothers used to torment me every time my parents' backs were turned.

From cutting my dolls' hair to mixing my makeup, I wanted to kill them all day, every day."

Justin laughed. "Ha! I had it just as bad. Yvonne used to change the time on the microwave whenever I heated up something. If I put it on two minutes, she'd change it to ten minutes. I'm surprised I still have any taste buds left after having burned them off so many times. And Jocelyn would always tamper with whatever electronic device I was building. Once, she rerouted the wires on a remote-controlled car I was working on. I almost burned my room down when I turned the damned thing on," he muttered.

Siobhan laughed so hard she sputtered and choked on her tea. She grabbed a napkin, wiped away the tears and fanned herself. "Your sisters are a mess."

Justin shook his head. "And don't get me started on dating."

"Oh, my goodness! *Yes.* They used to scare my dates so bad, those boys wouldn't give me a second look."

"How about inviting three girls over at the same time?"

Her mouth fell open. "I sure would've loved to see how you got out of that one."

"It wasn't easy. I couldn't get a date for six months after that little stunt."

They continued to laugh and swap stories over second and third cups of coffee and tea. Siobhan enjoyed every moment. When she finally glanced at her watch, three hours had passed. "I didn't realize how late it is. I'm supposed to be at my parents' house right now."

"I'm sorry. I didn't mean to make you late." He leaned forward and flashed that sexy smile. "But I have to tell you, this is the best non-date I've ever had."

The timbre of his voice and the intensity of his gaze made her pulse race. "I...I had a good time, too." She opened her purse and pulled out a few bills.

"What do you think you're doing?" Justin asked, staring at her as if she had lost her mind. "Siobhan, please put your money away. My invite, my dime."

She didn't want to owe any man or find strings attached to an invitation, so she always made it a practice to pay her own way, even for a three-dollar cup of tea. But Justin stared her down until she put the money back in her purse. "Thanks. I'd better go."

He was up and around to her side of the booth with his hand extended before she took her next breath. Recalling the warm feelings his touch stirred in her last night, she hesitated briefly before placing her hand in his. He gently helped Siobhan to her feet and tugged her close to him. For a moment she thought he might kiss her… She *wanted* him to kiss her.

Finally he backed away and murmured, "Let me pay for this and I'll walk you to your car." Justin gestured for her to lead the way to the counter.

She walked ahead of him on shaky legs, feeling the heat of his gaze on her. After paying, Justin reached for her hand again and pushed through the doors. They stopped next to her car.

"Nice ride," he said.

"Thanks. I like it," she said of the Lexus SUV. "I wanted a little luxury, but it had to be safe and functional, as well." They fell silent for a moment.

"Well, I guess I should let you go. Siobhan, I know you said you don't have time to date, but I'd really like to see you again. We can even come back here again, if you like."

"Justin, I—"

He moved his body flush against hers. "Please don't say no."

The contact made her pulse leap. She opened her mouth to tell him she couldn't see him, and his mouth came down on hers. He kissed her gently, unhurriedly, bringing his hands up to frame her face, holding her in place. A slow burn started in her belly and flared out to the other parts of her body, causing her to tremble. Siobhan moaned.

Justin eased back and whispered against her lips, "Say you'll go out with me." He gifted her with one last kiss and stepped back.

Still trying to get her breathing under control, she said, "Can I think about it?"

"Absolutely." He whipped out his cell. "Give me your number and I'll call you this week."

She recited the numbers then pressed the remote to unlock her doors. He reached around her and opened the door.

After she was seated behind the wheel, he leaned in and kissed her again. "Drive safely, and enjoy your dinner."

Siobhan managed to nod. She started the car with a shaky hand and backed out of the spot. Justin smiled and threw up a wave as she passed. She waved back and wondered what she was getting herself into.

For the second day in a row, Justin watched Siobhan drive away. He raked a hand down his face. He wasn't supposed to kiss her, only engage her in friendly conversation. He certainly hadn't planned to ask her out again. He walked to where his car was parked an aisle over, got in and leaned against the headrest. Her full, sexy lips were softer than he'd anticipated, and he could still taste the sweet flavor of honey from the kiss they'd shared. When she had scooped out the bit of honey left in the package with her finger and sucked it off, he almost came out of his seat. Justin had wanted to smear honey all over her and lick off every drop. If he ever got her to his house…

He shook the thought away. No honey and no more kisses. He needed to focus on the goal and not get distracted. Except he had just asked her out on a date. He groaned. What was he doing? Okay, maybe dinner, nice conversation and sharing more childhood stories. Nothing more. He could do that. He had never allowed a woman to stand in the way of his dreams, and he wouldn't now. Feeling confident he could pull it off, Justin started the engine and drove home.

Once there, he went directly to his home office, booted up the computer and worked on his in-home safety sensor program. An hour later he placed sensors in his living room and used his cell to test whether it would distinguish between heights.

"Yes!"

Now that he had solved that problem, he had only a couple more additions he wanted to make. He was close to having a system that would outperform his competitors. And if it hit the market in a big way…

Excitement raced through his veins. Justin's stomach rumbled. The toast and coffee was long gone. He removed the sensors, shut down the computer and padded to the kitchen to find something to eat.

After finishing his meal, he tried to concentrate on the basketball game he was watching, but thoughts of Siobhan continued to play in his mind. Although she laughed and talked, she seemed somewhat guarded, even a little tense at times. He had fully expected her to bolt after the first few minutes and was surprised but pleased she stayed as long as she had. Sitting here now, he realized Siobhan had revealed very little about herself, preferring to keep the subject focused on her family and him. He chuckled thinking back on some of the stories they'd shared, especially the ones about dating, and wondered if her brothers still ran interference. Not that he should care one way or the other. Dating Siobhan Hunter did not fall under the scope of his mission. Yet something about her made him want to peel back the layers to find out what lay beneath her prim exterior.

Justin glanced over at his cell and debated whether to call her. Was she still having dinner with family, or had she gone home to an empty house like him? Several minutes passed, and then he picked up the phone. It buzzed in his hand immediately.

"Hey, Joce. What's up? Your ears must have been burning."

"Hey, Justin. You were talking about me, huh? Hopefully it was to some cute guy."

He snorted. "In your dreams, Short Stack," he said, using the nickname he had given her when she was five.

"Hey, I may be short, but I've got my assets in all the right places," Jocelyn retorted.

Justin frowned. "I don't want to hear about your *assets*, and there'd better not be anybody else looking at them, either," he gritted out.

She laughed. "Oh, lighten up, big brother. I'm too busy right now to deal with guys. So, who were you telling about me?"

"I was sharing with a friend some of the pranks you and Yvonne used to pull. Turns out she had siblings who did her the same way."

"Did you say *she*? I haven't heard you talk about a woman in ages. Ooh, wait till I tell Yvonne."

"Slow your roll, girl. It's not like that. Anyway, I know you're not calling to get in my business, so what's on your mind?"

"We're working on a project in my engineering class, and I need your help."

"What kind of project?"

"Designing an intruder detection system. I'm having trouble with it differentiating between humans and pets. Right now it goes off anytime there's movement."

"Inside, outside or both?"

"Inside. It should work in any enclosed environment."

"Did you build in filters to minimize false positives and negatives?"

"I thought I did," she grumbled. "So, can you help?"

He really wanted to call Siobhan, but it would have to wait. He rose to his feet and walked to his office. "Yeah. Send me what you have and we'll work on it."

"Thanks, Justin! I'm going to put you on speaker so Alana and Francesca can hear."

"Who?"

"My partners. Those guys aren't going to know what hit them when we unveil this project," Jocelyn added with a giggle.

Justin shook his head and clicked on the email his sister had sent. He plugged in the cell, figuring the battery would be close to dead by the time the call ended if he didn't. He scanned the document. "All right. Let's see what you've got."

They went back and forth, and he talked them through a series of steps. He asked them several questions and was impressed by the wealth of knowledge all three young women possessed. Instead of using sensors, which an intruder could step over or avoid, they had chosen to use a camera and create a system with image processing. Later, Jocelyn assured him they could handle things, thanked him and hung up with a promise to let him know how the final project turned out.

He checked the time—five o'clock. Knowing he shouldn't, but unable to resist, Justin dialed Siobhan.

"Hello," came the tentative greeting when she answered.

"Siobhan, it's Justin."

"Oh. Hey."

"Did I catch you at a bad time?"

"We just finished cooking dinner and are about to take everything to the table."

"I'm sorry. I figured you'd be done with dinner."

"It's no problem. I usually come early to help with the cooking," Siobhan answered. "Was there something you wanted?"

"Yes. No." Justin felt like a sixteen-year-old again, calling a girl for the first time. What was wrong with him? "I just wanted you to know how much I enjoyed your company today, and I'm hoping you'll give me a chance to take you out on a real date."

Her soft laughter came through the line. "You're persistent, if nothing else."

He hadn't got this far in life without being tenacious, particularly when it came to pursuing his goals. "Only when necessary."

"I did say I'd think about it, but stalking me isn't going to win you any prizes or *dates*."

He chuckled. "Okay, so no stalking. Got it. What about kisses? Siobhan!" he called when she didn't answer.

"I'm here."

"Well?"

"Well, what?"

"My kisses. Will they win me any prizes or a date?"

"I have to go, Justin."

"You're not going to answer my question?"

"No, I am not," she whispered. "Goodbye."

"I'll talk to you later." Justin drummed his fingers on the desk. He had no idea what possessed him to flirt with her that way. His common sense seemed to take a hike each time he heard her voice. Canceling the date would be the best thing, but he didn't see that happening, either.

Chapter 4

Siobhan clutched the phone to her chest and drew in a deep, steadying breath. Hearing Justin's smooth-as-velvet voice brought back everything his kisses made her feel with vivid clarity—feelings she had spent the past three hours trying to forget. Why hadn't she declined that second date?

"Siobhan, are you planning to bring that mac and cheese to the table sometime today, or are you going to stand there daydreaming?"

She whirled around at the sound of her mother's voice and shoved the cell into her jeans pocket. "I'm coming right now." She grabbed the dish and rushed off to the dining room.

"Is everything all right, honey?" her mother asked, following behind Siobhan and placing a platter filled with sliced prime rib, turkey and ham on the table. "You looked a little troubled after that phone call."

She shifted uncomfortably under her mother's scrutiny.

"I'm fine. Just talking to a friend." She glanced back at the table laden with all manner of food. "I think that's about it. I'll go let everybody know."

Lively chatter commenced as her family gathered around the table. There was a brief pause in the conversation while her father blessed the food, and then it started up again as everyone filled his or her plate.

"Siobhan, that's all you're eating?" Siobhan's only sister, Morgan, asked. "Usually, three-fourths of your plate is covered with macaroni and cheese."

Siobhan glanced down at her half-empty plate. Macaroni and cheese was her absolute favorite food, but thoughts of Justin still had her stomach in knots. "I'm just not that hungry."

"Did you eat with your friend earlier?" her mother asked.

Brandon turned her way. "What friend?"

Siobhan rolled her eyes. "I just met a friend for coffee."

"It wouldn't happen to be one of the men I saw you dancing with last night?"

"Really, Brandon? All those men wanted to pitch their latest product. I don't know why they didn't just talk to you or Daddy."

"In case you haven't noticed, Dad's a little intimidating, and you're way prettier than Brandon," Khalil said with a chuckle.

"Whatever," she said.

"Does that include the guy you danced with twice and who walked you out?" Brandon asked mildly after taking a sip of his tea.

She leveled him with an angry stare. "I can't believe you. What, were you following me or something?"

"Just answer the question."

"None of your business," Siobhan snapped.

"Brandon, leave your sister alone," her mother interrupted. "Was he a nice young man, Siobhan?"

Siobhan groaned inwardly. DeAnna Gray was on a mission to see all of her children happily married, and with Siobhan being the oldest, her mother thought she should set the example. Siobhan shrugged. "He was nice enough, but as I said, they all just really wanted an in to the company."

"You know, there was this one young man I met last night," her father started. "He had a great idea. I told him to call the office and get on my schedule."

"Did you recognize him, Dad?" Brandon asked.

"No. He said his name was—"

Her mother held up her hand. "All right, all right. That's enough. There will be no business talk at the dinner table." The rule had been in place as far back as Siobhan could remember.

Her father nodded. "You're right, Anna."

The conversation shifted to Malcolm's upcoming vacation. He usually took a monthlong retreat in the spring before he had to start football training camp in late summer. "I'm looking forward to getting away for a while. And I've never been to Belize, so it should be fun."

"Too bad we're getting ready for the new product release. I'd really like to go with you," Siobhan said.

"Me, too," Morgan added. "I haven't had time to even think about a vacation." Morgan worked in the company's legal department, joining right out of law school two years ago.

Malcolm smiled. "Vonnie, I'm sure Dad wouldn't mind giving you two a few days off. Brandon, on the other hand…" He shook his head.

Everyone burst into laughter. Siobhan put in hours well above what was considered normal, but Brandon was a true workaholic.

Brandon waved a hand dismissively. "Whatever, boy. At least I have a real job, instead of running down a field with a ball and working less than half a year. And I take *plenty* of time to play."

The usual argument ensued about who worked harder, drawing Khalil, a former model turned fitness buff, into the discussion. Siobhan and Morgan shared a smile, shook their heads and resumed eating.

Later, while putting food away, Morgan asked, "So, you met a guy at the fund-raiser last night?"

"I met several. One was older than Grandpa, two were trying so hard to impress me that they stuttered and babbled like idiots, and one had bathed in some foul-smelling concoction that was supposed to be cologne, and it was all I could do not to pass out. They all tried to ask me out and pitch their idea in one breath. Lately, those are the only men I seem to attract."

Morgan laughed. "Sounds like you had a fun night. I'm glad I didn't go. Which one was the guy Brandon mentioned? The one you danced with twice and walked you out. What was his angle?"

"Neither. Actually, Justin and I just danced." She spooned the remaining potato salad into the container and put on the lid. "I met him at a café downtown this morning."

"Ah. So that's why you rushed me off the phone. How'd it go?"

Siobhan shrugged. "Okay, I guess. He asked me out again, but I don't know."

"Was he a nice guy?"

"Yeah. He seems nice enough, so far." She recalled the three hours they spent talking and laughing. She couldn't remember the last time she had spent so much time simply sitting and talking with a man. And enjoying it.

"If he's nice, go for it. You deserve someone better than Arthur." Morgan wrinkled her nose as if she smelled something bad. "I couldn't stand him. I wish you had let the brothers kick his butt like they wanted to. He had it coming after what he did to you. Did you ever get your money back?"

Siobhan cringed at the mention of her ex. "Only some of it. He had already invested five thousand in the scam that went belly-up, and he wasted the rest. Getting my money back would've meant filing a suit, a public battle and more people in my business. I just wanted it all to go away." It had taken her two years of dedication to grow her savings account again.

Morgan placed stacked containers into bags for each of them—her mother insisted—and the others into the refrigerator. "Well, hopefully Justin doesn't turn out to be a jerk. I assume since he was at the banquet last night that he's in the safety business."

"He said he has a couple of products on the market, but we didn't really talk about it. We talked mostly about growing up with annoying siblings."

"Hey!" Morgan said with mock outrage. "I was *not* annoying."

Siobhan laughed. "Not too often. And you were my only ally against the boys."

"Tell me about it."

Malcolm came into the kitchen. "Uh-oh. What are you two in here plotting?"

"Nothing, big head," Morgan said and handed him a bag.

"Thanks. You ready to leave?"

"Yep."

Siobhan shook her head. "You rode with him on that motorcycle?"

Morgan grinned. "But of course. You should try it."

"No, thanks. I prefer having a little more metal surrounding me."

Malcolm kissed Siobhan's cheek. "It's fun, and I'm a

safe driver. Whenever you want to ride, let me know. I'll go extra slow."

"I'll pass." Siobhan and Morgan hugged. "Be safe, you two."

"We will," they chorused.

She smiled at the twins as they exited. Morgan had always been a daredevil, just like her twin, and thought she should be able to do anything Malcolm did, including playing football. Good thing it wasn't allowed in the NFL; otherwise Morgan might give him a run for his money. Siobhan finished up in the kitchen, said her goodbyes and headed home.

She put in a couple of hours of work before going to bed, and she was up and in the office by six thirty the next morning working on the press kit for the new pressure-distribution mattress the company would be unveiling in two weeks. The test subjects had raved over the comfort, usability and ease of care as compared to other same type of mattresses, and the marketing team had done a great job generating public interest.

Siobhan spoke with the production manager to make sure the mattress would be ready as scheduled, checked with the marketing manager for copies of the new brochure and the website designer to make sure it had been updated. At nine, she made her way one floor down to the conference room for the weekly staff meeting. She greeted those already seated, placed her folders on the table and went to get a cup of coffee. Siobhan didn't drink coffee often, but since they had purchased a Keurig Brewing System, she allowed herself one cup of Mocha Swirl each week.

Minutes later, her father called the meeting to order. Siobhan listened to the announcements and updates. She nearly jumped out of her skin when her cell buzzed in the pocket of her suit jacket. In her haste to get to the meeting, she had forgotten to put it on Silent. She pulled it out and her hand froze midswipe. She knew she should just turn it off until the meeting concluded, but seeing the text from Justin piqued her curiosity, and she clicked on the message.

When I woke up this morning, you were the first thing on my mind. I hope you're thinking about me, too. I'll call you later to discuss our first date. I can't wait to see you again.

She closed her eyes and tried to ignore the excitement that raced through her. The last thing she needed was to let a simple text message get under her skin.

"Siobhan?"

Her father's voice broke into her thoughts, and her eyes snapped open. The woman next to her whispered that it was Siobhan's turn to give an update. Siobhan pulled herself together and presented her information, but for the remainder of the meeting she couldn't keep her mind off Justin. After the meeting, Brandon cornered her.

"You okay, sis?"

"Fine. Just focused on making sure we're ready to go public with the new mattress."

He nodded. "I heard you've been here from early morning to late at night. You need to delegate."

"No. This is my job and I'm not going to let Daddy down." One of her greatest fears had always been disappointing her parents. As the oldest, Siobhan felt it was her responsibility to set the example. Her stomach constricted with the memory of the one time she'd slipped.

"Delegating isn't letting Dad down. It's keeping your sanity. Take it from me. I know." He squeezed her shoulder. "Stop trying to do it all. I'll see you later."

She watched him go, then gathered up her belongings.

"Mr. Cohen never had to be called twice in a meeting."

Siobhan slowly turned to face Gordon Samuels. The fortysomething-year-old man worked in her department and made it no secret that he didn't think Siobhan could handle the PR director position. He had voiced on several occasions all the reasons he should have been appointed to the position when Mr. Cohen retired a year ago, including the fact that he had worked for the company three years longer than Siobhan. She took in the rumpled suit that looked as if it had been slept in, the crooked tie that didn't match anything he had on and the grease stain on the front of his white shirt. She wanted to stand him in front of a mirror. While Gordon came up with some good ideas, there was no way she'd ever allow him to be the face of her family's company. Image was everything, and his... She shook her head.

"Is there something you want to say to me?" Siobhan asked.

"The only reason you're in this position is because your father owns the company. That job should've been mine," he gritted out.

"Whatever you say, Gordon." Rather than stoop to his level, she just shook her head and walked out. She had more pressing things to deal with, like finding a way to decline that date with Justin. With Gordon gunning for her job, she had to stay on her toes. And that meant not being distracted by the mahogany Adonis.

Justin poured a second cup of coffee, hoping it would give him the jolt he needed, and took it outside to sip while sitting on the back deck. He'd lain awake for most of the night thinking about Siobhan and how much he wanted to kiss her again. Even his morning run had done nothing to clear his mind. He had sent her a text, but she hadn't replied. Not that he thought she would.

Even though she had seemed to enjoy their time together, she kept the ironclad control wrapped around her like a protective armor. Did she ever let her guard down enough to have some fun? And what would she be like if she let go? Downing the last of the liquid, he stood and went back inside to call Gray Home Safety. With any luck, he'd be able to get on the schedule by the end of the week. Justin retrieved the card from his office desk and punched in the number. Minutes later, he hung up, disappointed. The earliest appointment wasn't for three weeks. In a way, it was a good thing since he still had a few things that he needed to work on. Now that the fog surrounding his brain had lifted, he went to work.

Justin's focus held for the first hour, but thoughts of Siobhan slowly crept into the forefront of his mind. She had probably started her workday, and if her job was as hectic as she said, he didn't expect to hear from her anytime soon. Pushing the speculations aside, he shifted back into work mode, alternating between typing codes and testing the sensors. By the time he looked up again, more than three hours had passed. He leaned back in the chair and closed his eyes. He had been staring at the computer screen for so long the letters and numbers started to blur. Justin rubbed a hand across his forehead and rose to his feet. His cell rang in midstretch. A smile creased his face when he saw Siobhan's name on the screen.

"Good afternoon, Ms. Hunter."

There was a slight pause before she said, "Good afternoon, Justin."

"Did you get my text?"

"Yes, but it's been a busy day, so I'm just able to return your call."

"So?"

"So what?"

"Were you thinking of me this morning, too?"

"I thought you wanted to discuss going on a date."

Justin chuckled. She didn't let up for a second. "I do, but—"

"Okay. I propose we go back to the same coffee shop."

"I was thinking of some place a little more upscale, like a real restaurant," he said wryly.

"The coffee shop is fine. I can meet you there Wednesday or Thursday."

"And I can pick you up."

"That won't be necessary. I'll most likely be leaving from work, so it just makes more sense for me to meet you there rather than driving home first."

When he dated a woman, he made it a practice to pick her up and take her back home, but Siobhan wouldn't budge in her position, so Justin reluctantly agreed. "Okay. How about Wednesday at seven?"

"Let's make it seven thirty to be safe. I hate being late."

"That works."

"I have to get back to work."

"Have a nice afternoon, Siobhan. I can't wait to see you."

"Goodbye, Justin. And, yes, I thought about you," Siobhan added, so softly that he almost missed it.

Justin smiled. Maybe he'd get that date after all.

Justin stared at Siobhan over the rim of his glass. His gaze dropped down to her near-empty salad plate and then back up to her face. It had taken a lot of convincing on his part to get her to order more than tea. And, just like last time, she kept the conversation on general topics and deflected any personal questions he asked. But he wanted to know more about *her*. He took a sip of his Coke then set the glass down. "What do you like to do for fun, Siobhan?"

Siobhan lowered her eyes to her plate. "I don't have much time for fun. My job keeps me extremely busy."

"I get that, but on those rare times that you're not busy, what do you do—dance, bowl, stand on tabletops and sing…?"

She burst out laughing, and the warm, throaty sound hit him like a ton of bricks. Her eyes sparkled, and the tense lines around her face relaxed. *"Stand on tabletops and sing?"*

Justin shrugged. "Just asking."

"No, I do not sing on tabletops."

"Well, you didn't say anything, so I was left to my own imagination."

She rolled her eyes, but was still smiling. "For your information, I like going to the movies and the beach."

"What kind of movies? Chick flicks?"

"Yes, but I'm not opposed to a good action film."

"What was the last movie you saw?"

Siobhan's brows knit. "Honestly, I don't remember. It's been a while."

"Then it's a good thing we met. Sounds like you need to get out more." He gestured to her now-empty plate. "Do you want anything else? Dessert?"

"No, thank you. I really should get going. There are a couple of things I need to wrap up tonight, and I have an early morning tomorrow."

Justin downed the remainder of his drink and signaled for the waiter. He paid the bill and walked Siobhan to her car. "Is your office open on the weekends?"

"No. Why?"

"I was hoping we could go to dinner at a *restaurant*. It's been a while since I've gone to the movies, and I thought we could do that, too."

"Justin, I—"

"You just said you're not working on the weekend, and I enjoy being with you."

"I've enjoyed these times with you, but right now my job is my priority."

"Siobhan, I don't plan to interfere with your job because

mine is a priority, as well. One dinner and a movie—then we'll see how it goes from there. What do you say?"

"All right."

He smiled. "And this time I'm picking you up and bringing you home."

Justin thought she would argue, but she nodded instead. "Thank you."

He pulled out his cell and handed it to her so she could input her address. "I should probably follow you home. It's getting late."

Siobhan lifted an eyebrow. "You're taking this gentleman thing a little far, aren't you?"

"Nope." He slanted his mouth over hers, inhaling her reply. His arm slid around her waist and pulled her closer to the fit of his body. Justin could have kept right on kissing her, but didn't want to press his luck. He stepped back, held the car door open and waited for her to get in. "I'll be right behind you," he said, closing the door.

He slid into his car and gripped the steering wheel. Each kiss he gave Siobhan challenged his resolve to keep their relationship casual.

Chapter 5

"Damn!" That was the second mistake Justin had made today. He'd got a late start due to an overnight power outage, and he had to wait for all his electronic devices to charge. Now he couldn't stop thinking about Siobhan and their date last night. After following her home, he'd had a hard time not jumping out of his car and seeing if he could persuade her to let him come inside for a while. But he knew if he had, they would have ended up in her bed, and that was the last thing either of them needed. If he didn't get back on track, the alert system wouldn't be ready to present to Mr. Gray. And he refused to blow an opportunity he'd been waiting for.

Less than an hour later, his doorbell rang, interrupting his flow. Justin groaned. "What now?" he muttered and stomped to the front door. He snatched it open.

"Surprise!"

Yvonne and Jocelyn stood on the porch with wide grins. His frown immediately disappeared, and a smile took its place. "What are you two doing here?" he asked, opening the door wider and engulfing them in a big hug. "Come on in." They followed him to the family room, and he sat in his favorite recliner.

Yvonne kicked off her shoes and dropped down on the sofa. "I took the day off. Joce and I had lunch and she told me about your new girlfriend, so…" She let the sentence hang, as if that were explanation enough.

Justin threw a look at Jocelyn, who entered the room from the kitchen, carrying a glass of water. "I thought I told you it wasn't like that."

Jocelyn sat next to her sister on the sofa and shrugged. "Well, you are known for lying about your relationships. So who is she, and what does she look like? You have any pictures?"

"Ooh, yeah. What does she do? She does have a job, right?" Yvonne asked with a raised eyebrow.

He groaned. "You two do realize that you're not nine and thirteen anymore. And what makes you think I'd tell you anything about my relationships after all the trouble you caused me?"

"I forgot all about that," Yvonne said with a laugh. "It was pretty comical watching you try to explain to three girls that you didn't invite them over."

Jocelyn joined in the laughter. "The look on your face was priceless." She tried to do an imitation of the shocked expression Justin knew he must have had when he had walked into their parents' living room and seen the three girls there, but failed because she was laughing too hard.

Justin scowled at his sisters as they continued to laugh. "If you came over here just to laugh at me all over again, you both can leave."

"I'm sorry," Jocelyn said, trying to catch her breath. "Seriously though, we wouldn't do something like that now. We just want to know if she makes you happy."

Yvonne nodded.

He divided his gaze between them. "I don't know if she makes me happy or not. We just met and have only gone out twice to a little coffee shop."

Yvonne's eyes lit up. "So you *do* have a new girlfriend."

"No, I do not. It's completely laid-back. She's really busy with her job, and I'm trying to get my alert system ready to present to a home-safety company. That doesn't leave either of us much time for a long-term relationship. I have plenty of time to settle down."

She waved him off. "Oh, please. It's called balance, Justin. Chris and I have been dating for six months, and we're both busy with our jobs, too. But we make time for each other. It doesn't have to be one or the other."

Justin's scowl deepened. "Chris? Who the hell is Chris? And why haven't I met him, Yvonne Marie Cartwright?"

Yvonne shared a look with Jocelyn, and they both rolled their eyes. "Here we go again," Yvonne said. "As you pointed out, *Justin Antonio Cartwright*, we are not nine and thirteen anymore. We are grown women and have active dating lives."

"You should try it," Jocelyn added with a smirk. "It might improve your productivity."

He jumped to his feet. He couldn't handle this conversation. Okay, it might be irrational to hold on to the notion that his sisters were still wide-eyed, innocent little girls, but to consider the alternative nearly made his heart stop. He shook his head. "I don't want to hear this."

Jocelyn chuckled. "Good, because we're not here to talk about us. What did you say your girlfriend's name was again?"

"I don't think he ever said, Joce." Yvonne looked at Justin and, giving him her most charming smile, said, "Her name is…"

Justin threw up his hands. He knew he was fighting a

losing battle with these two, especially since they'd decided to double-team him. If he wanted a moment of peace sometime in the next century, it would be in his best interest to surrender and tell them what they wanted to know. "Her name is Siobhan Hunter, and we've only known each other a week." He shook his head at their twin smiles of victory. "Go home," he said, trying to hide his own smile.

"We really hope she turns out to be the one. I can't wait to be an aunt."

"Me, either, Yvonne. I talked to Mom the other day, and she said she hoped Justin settled down soon so she could have some grandbabies."

This was definitely not a conversation he wanted to have. Justin spun on his heel and retreated to the safety of his office to work on his program. But Yvonne's words continued to play around the fringes of his mind: *We really hope she turns out to be the one.* Did he hope for the same? He kept telling himself no, but if that were the case, why was Siobhan the first thing on his mind when he woke up and the last thing when he closed his eyes at night?

Siobhan sat in her office Friday holding her cell phone and debating—for the second day in a row—whether to cancel her Saturday-night date with Justin. She didn't want to give him any false hope about them starting a relationship, especially after what had happened last time. Her heart constricted with the painful memory of overhearing Arthur's plans to get his hands on Siobhan's company shares for some shady business deal. But what hurt her most was hearing him on the phone telling another woman he loved her, and that as soon as he had Siobhan's money, the two of them could get married. Without a second thought, Siobhan had canceled the wedding three weeks before the date, even though the invitations had gone out and the gifts had started to arrive. She couldn't put herself or her family through that kind of disappointment again. She needed to focus all her energy on excelling in her job. Gordon was waiting for her to mess up, and she refused to give him one ounce of ammunition against her.

Making a decision, Siobhan found Justin's phone number and took a deep breath. Her finger hovered over the call button for several seconds before she changed her mind and sent a quick text message. If she heard his voice, she knew he could easily persuade her to change her mind— another reason why she couldn't go out with him. The cell buzzed in her hand, and her pulse skipped. Siobhan relaxed upon seeing Kendra's text letting her know she and Cynthia were downstairs waiting for their lunch date. She sent a reply, tossed the cell in her purse and left to meet them.

Siobhan exited the elevator and spotted her two friends in the lobby area. "Sorry I'm late," she said as she approached. "I have a ton of stuff on my desk and lost track of time. I don't have a lot of time, so I was hoping we could eat in the café here." She gestured to the other side of the lobby. Sweet Delights Café had been open only six months and served breakfast and lunch.

"As long as the food is good, it works for me," Kendra said. "What about you, Cyn?"

"It's fine."

They started toward the café entrance. "It's almost one, so we should have missed the lunch crowd," Siobhan said. A woman greeted them and directed the trio to a table.

As soon as they placed their orders, Cynthia asked, "So, how's it going with Justin? Has he asked you out yet?"

Siobhan knew this would be the first question. "I met him twice at a coffee shop near the hotel where we had the fund-raiser."

Kendra rolled her eyes. "Met him? I can't believe the brother didn't even pick you up. Judging by the way he behaved that night, I thought for sure he would know how to treat a woman."

"I was the one who insisted on meeting him there," Siobhan confessed. "Justin did offer to pick me up. He actually asked me out to dinner and a movie tomorrow, but I just canceled."

Kendra laughed. "The first two dates were that bad?"

She sighed. "No. We had a really good time. He's funny, charming…"

"Then what's your problem, girl?" Cynthia asked.

"I don't want him to get any ideas that this might be headed somewhere, so I figured it was better to nip it in the bud before we went any further." The server returned and placed their food on the table. Siobhan picked up her fork and stabbed at the salad.

Kendra pointed a French fry toward Siobhan. "You know you're wrong punishing Justin for Arthur's mess."

"I'm not trying to punish him." True, she had no desire to put her heart on the line again, but more than that, being with Justin made her feel things she couldn't explain, things that frightened her.

"Justin sounds like a great guy, and you owe it to yourself to be happy," Cynthia said. "At least let him mess up before you toss him aside. You should call him back and tell him you'll be free tomorrow after all. I know you haven't seen a movie since the last one the three of us went to—a *year* ago."

She opened her mouth to refute Cynthia, then closed it. A frown creased her brow. Had that been the last movie she'd seen?

"See, you know I'm right. Every time I call you, you're at that office—day, night or even some weekends, when it's supposed to be closed. Life is passing you by, Siobhan."

"Cynthia's right, Siobhan. Ever since the accident, you haven't been the same. That carefree girl who loved life went away, and in her place is this serious woman who rarely laughs, never wants to go out and is always working."

Siobhan straightened her shoulders. "Sometimes you have to sacrifice certain things when you're not a kid anymore and have responsibilities. Life isn't always about being spontaneous and having fun."

"But sometimes it is," Kendra said, popping another fry into her mouth. She finished chewing and continued. "No one is saying you should neglect your job, run off and act like you don't have obligations. We all have jobs, but it's okay to let your hair down and have some real fun every now and again."

They ate in silence while Siobhan contemplated her friend's comments. Had she really become such a serious and boring person? Admittedly, she worked a lot, but they didn't understand the pressure of being the oldest and having to set the example for her siblings.

"You're going to call Justin back and tell him you'll go, right?" Kendra asked as they were finishing their meals.

"Probably not." As much as Siobhan enjoyed their mini dates, she couldn't let herself be drawn into another relationship where she might end up with her heart broken again. She placed her napkin on the table. "I need to get back."

"Okay. It's my turn to pay, so go ahead," Cynthia said. "What day are we meeting next week?"

Kendra pulled out her phone and accessed the calendar. "I can do Wednesday or Friday."

Siobhan checked hers. "Wednesday works for me. Can we go around one? I have a meeting at eleven with my staff, and although it should only last an hour, with Gordon and his constant complaints, who knows how long it'll last."

"Is he still mad because you got the director's job?" Kendra asked with surprise. "That was over a year ago."

She pushed her chair back and stood. "Yes. He's just waiting for me to make one little mistake, and I have to stay on top of my game, which is another reason I don't have time for a relationship."

"Don't forget my anniversary party next Friday," Kendra said. "You should bring Justin."

"I don't think so. I have to go." They agreed to a time and place for lunch next week, and Siobhan headed back to her office.

She worked steadily throughout the afternoon and into the evening, stopping only once to get a cup of green tea.

"Time to pack up and go home, Siobhan."

She glanced up to see Brandon standing in the doorway with his arms folded. "I still have a few more things to do. Are you leaving?"

"Yes, and so are you. It's almost eight." Brandon straightened his tall frame and walked into the office. "You can wipe that frown off your face because it doesn't work on me. Now pack it up and let's go."

Siobhan glared at him, and he had the nerve to smile. "In case you forgot, *I'm* the oldest. And I see you're still here."

"I was only here waiting for you."

"Why? I don't need a babysitter."

"That's debatable," he muttered.

"I heard that."

"Good—now come on. I'm supposed to be meeting Khalil and Malcolm at the gym to play basketball in thirty minutes."

"Then don't let me keep you."

Brandon released a deep sigh. "Vonnie, you have five minutes to get your stuff or I'm calling Dad. You know what he said."

Siobhan jumped to her feet. "Seriously, Brandon. That's just wrong." Their father had told them on several occasions that there was more to life than working, and that he didn't want them staying at the office past normal business hours on a regular basis. Of course, he'd fussed at Siobhan already four times in the past two weeks.

He pulled out his cell. "What's it going to be?"

She rolled her eyes and started shoving folders in her tote bag, all the while muttering about what he could do with his threat. She slung the tote on her shoulder and stormed past him. "And lock my door."

He chuckled and followed her out. As they rode down in the elevator, he asked, "Are you still seeing that guy from the fund-raiser?"

His question reminded her that Justin had never responded to her text. Had he got it, or was he purposely ignoring her? She felt bad about canceling, but it couldn't be helped. "I saw him a couple of times. It's no big thing."

"If you say so. I'm telling you now, if he pulls the same crap as Arthur, we're kicking his ass. We backed off because you asked us to last time, but we won't stand for someone hurting you again."

"Since I don't plan to start seeing him exclusively, you have nothing to worry about."

They exited the elevator in the underground garage, and he walked Siobhan to her car. Bending slightly, he placed a kiss on her temple. "Just be careful."

"I will. Tell Khalil I'll try to get in there one evening next week, if he's going to be there."

"I can come work out with you, if he's busy. Just let me know."

"I will. See you later." Siobhan got in the car, started it and backed out of the lot. She shook her head. It had taken days of pleading and threatening to tell their parents to keep her three brothers from killing Arthur. They could be an intimidating group. But somehow, Justin didn't strike her as the type who would scare easily.

She dismissed the wayward thought immediately. She needed to focus on work only. No more dates—and definitely no more kisses.

Siobhan sat at her kitchen table late Saturday afternoon working on the press release and tweaking the ads that would be sent to various magazines and newspapers in the coming week. After reading and reworking the release three times, she was finally satisfied with the finished product. Just as she hit the print button, her doorbell rang. She figured it was one of her brothers. Anytime a man showed interest in her or Morgan, the guys each paid a visit to interrogate their sisters. She made her way to the front door and snatched it open without looking through the peephole.

"Look, I don't…" Her eyes widened and her sentence trailed off. "Justin. What…what are you doing here?" She had forgotten she'd given him her address.

"Can I come in?"

She hesitated for a split second before backing up and waving him in. She closed the door and leaned against it. His gaze burned a slow path down her body and back up, and Siobhan felt a sudden need to cover herself.

"Nice outfit."

Since she didn't have plans to leave the house, she'd put on a tank top and an old pair of cutoff jean shorts that revealed more than they covered. "I wasn't expecting company, so… Anyway, you never answered my question."

"You canceled our date…by *text*," Justin said, as if that explained it all. "Why?"

If anything, she had expected him to call in response to her text, not show up at her house. "I told you—I have a lot of work I have to finish."

"It's Saturday, Siobhan." He closed the distance between

them, braced one hand on the door above her head and brought his face within six inches of hers. "You're going to have to do better than that, baby."

Siobhan's breath caught, and her pulse spiked.

"Did I say or do something wrong?"

She shook her head.

"I thought we had a good time both times at the coffee shop."

"Yes, but—"

"But what? When two people enjoy each other's company, it seems logical that they'd want to spend more time together."

"Justin, I think you're a really nice guy, but I don't want to lead you on or give you the impression I want anything from you other than friendship."

A slow grin tilted the corners of his mouth. "And you think by us going to dinner and a movie, I'll think you want more than friendship."

Siobhan nodded.

"What if I promise I won't assume you want anything other than a good time? Then will you go out with me?"

"What about you? What do you want?"

"All I want is to spend the evening with a beautiful woman." Justin eased close enough for their breaths to mingle. "So, Ms. Hunter, will you go out with me?"

With his lips so near and his eyes locked on hers, Siobhan could barely form a coherent thought, let alone answer him. Everything inside her screamed *no*, but she heard herself answer, "Yes," just before his mouth came crashing down on hers. Unlike the previous kisses they had shared, this one was more urgent and demanding. She felt her control slipping and pulled back.

"I made reservations for six thirty," he whispered against her lips. "That way we'll have plenty of time to see one of the later showings at the theater."

Still trying to get her heart rate under control, she said, "I need to change my clothes."

He moved back.

"You can wait in here." She led him to the family room. "Can I get you something to drink?"

Justin took a seat on her recliner. "No, thank you. This is really nice. Did you decorate it yourself?"

"With a little help from my sister." She had chosen neutral beiges and tans with splashes of coral to complement the stone fireplace. "I'll be right back."

In her bedroom, Siobhan paced and rubbed her temples. "What are you doing, Siobhan?" she mumbled. "All it took was a stupid kiss, and you're going back on your word." But damn, the man could kiss.

She stopped pacing and went to her closet. He said he didn't expect anything but some fun and an enjoyable evening. She could do this…as long as he kept his lips to himself.

Chapter 6

"Now, wasn't this better than the coffee shop?" Justin asked, leaning back in his chair after they finished their meal.

Siobhan scanned the upscale steak house with its elegant furnishings and intimate atmosphere. Several couples sat across from each other holding hands and sharing smiles. There wasn't an empty table in the place. "It's very nice, but how did you get reservations on such short notice?"

He took a sip of his wine. "I made reservations two days ago."

She angled her head. "You kept the original reservation, even after I canceled?"

"Yes."

"A little presumptuous, don't you think? And why didn't you respond to my message?"

"Not at all." Justin leaned forward and reached for her hand. "As far as not responding, I had hoped that by coming to your house, I could convince you to reconsider. I can't tell you how glad I am that you changed your mind, Siobhan."

The timbre of his voice, the way he said her name and the way he touched her had Siobhan's heart racing a mile a minute. Not wanting him to know how much he affected her, she eased her hand away and took a sip of her wine. "Like I told you before, you're persistent, if nothing else."

Justin chuckled. "Only when necessary."

They shared a smile, both remembering that particular conversation.

"Do you ever let go and just do something spontaneous? Maybe that one thing you always wanted to do, but haven't."

"No," she answered immediately. "With my schedule, I don't have room for *spontaneity*."

"Then what do you do for fun?"

If she could recall the last time she did something fun, she might have been able to answer his question. "I hang out with my family and best friends." Outside of the monthly family dinners and weekly lunches with her two friends, she couldn't come up with anything else that would qualify. Once she had handled that mess with Arthur, Siobhan had completely shut down her personal life. Not wanting to talk about her life anymore, she shifted the conversation. "You said your parents live outside of Las Vegas. Is that where you grew up?"

Justin smiled knowingly. "No. I grew up right here in Los Angeles. They moved there two years ago when the environmental consulting firm my father works for relocated. He said he was too close to retirement to start over. My mother is a librarian, and she said as long as they had books, she'd be fine."

Siobhan laughed. "I know you mentioned one of your sisters worked in forensics and the other one was in college. Are they here?"

"Yep. Yvonne works in the Long Beach Police Department crime lab, and Jocelyn is at UCLA. As a matter of fact, they paid me a surprise visit on Thursday. So, what were you doing in Las Vegas?"

Usually Siobhan had no problems directing the attention away from her, but Justin wasn't so easily put off. He kept finding a way to turn the conversation back to her personal life. "My two friends and I went to celebrate after graduating from college several years ago."

"That had to be a blast."

"Well, it would've been if Kendra hadn't got food poisoning. We ended up coming back home after a day and a half, and didn't get to explore the shops or see any shows."

"That's a shame. A lot has changed since then."

"I know. That's why I want to go back someday."

"Making that happen would require you to take some time off for *fun*, you know," Justin said with amusement.

She leveled him with a glare that was known to silence and send grown men scurrying, but it seemingly had no effect on him.

"It could be an entirely different city by the time you go back. I'm just saying," he added with a laugh when she narrowed her eyes. He glanced down at his watch. "We'd better get going if we want to catch a movie." He signaled the waiter and settled the bill, then stood.

"What are we going to see?"

"I have no idea," he said, helping Siobhan to her feet and guiding her to the exit. "I thought we'd decide once we got there. I'm not even sure what's playing right now."

"I guess I'm not the only one who hasn't been out in a while," she mumbled.

Justin laughed heartily. He leaned over and gave her a quick kiss. "You got me on that one."

Siobhan tried hard not to smile, but failed. Her smile was still in place as they drove to the movie theater.

"I guess everybody else had the same idea," he said as he drove around the lot searching for a parking place. He maneuvered into a recently vacated spot, hopped out and came around to Siobhan's side. He gently pulled her to her feet, entwined their hands and headed for the ticket booth. "Let's hope they have something good showing."

After staring at the selections for ten minutes, they finally settled on a show. They stopped short when they entered.

"Wow," Siobhan said.

"Yeah, wow. When did all this happen? I guess it has been a long time since I've been to the movies."

Siobhan chuckled. "For real." The lobby held a full bar, booths and an area for patrons to wait until their movie was called. Inside the theater, she was amazed once more at the large leather reclining seats—all reserved seating—and in-movie dining service. When the movie started, the suspense thriller had Siobhan nearly jumping out of her seat almost instantly.

Justin slung an arm around her shoulders and whispered, "If you don't like it, we can choose something else."

She shook her head and turned to reply at the same time he moved, and their lips brushed across each other, the brief contact sending sparks of pleasure through her. Siobhan waited for him to take full advantage, but he sat unmoving, then backed away.

"What were you going to say?"

It took her a second to get her scattered thoughts together. "I…I was going to say, it's okay—I'm fine. We don't have to leave."

He nodded. "Let me know if you change your mind."

"All right." Their gazes locked for several heated moments before she tore hers away and focused on the screen.

Throughout the movie, each time she jumped or made a sound, Justin tightened his arm around her. He lifted the armrest between them, and by the time the ending credits rolled, she was sitting halfway on his lap. It should have bothered her, especially since she wanted to keep the boundaries of friendship intact. But it didn't. No matter how hard she tried, she couldn't dismiss the fact that she liked the feeling of his strong arm surrounding her. And it unnerved her.

Justin kept stealing glances at Siobhan as he drove her home. She sat quietly and stared out the window. He couldn't figure her out. One moment she seemed relaxed and open, and in the next she'd retreated behind that impenetrable wall again. He knew she wanted him as much as he wanted her—her eyes and her kiss told him—but every time he made a little progress in getting to know her, she shut him down cold. Like the other two times they had gone out, whenever he asked her a personal question, she skirted around it and kept the attention on him.

Justin had never had to work this hard to gain a woman's interest, and maybe it was time he pulled back. It sounded like a logical step in theory; however, there was one flaw with his thinking—kissing her had been the only thing on his mind since their lips had accidentally touched. And he didn't see himself leaving without satisfying his craving. His groin stirred, and he gripped the steering wheel tighter. Needing a distraction, he turned up the music. Smooth R & B music flowed from his satellite radio station. "Is the music too loud? I can change the station if you don't like this one."

"Please. I love R & B. My parents love music, so we listened to R & B, jazz, gospel and even some classical. They have tons of albums and records."

"That's something else we have in common. My parents still listen to their albums on one of those old console stereos, static and all. Sometimes they have to turn the switch on and off a couple of times for it to work, but I can't get them to buy another one."

Siobhan laughed. "We bought our parents an updated stereo system about three years ago. Otherwise they would still have theirs."

Justin stroked his chin. "Maybe I need to do the same. Their anniversary is coming up in a few months."

"Ooh, I love this song," Siobhan said, tapping her fingers to the beat of "You Rock My World."

Justin smiled. "You're a Michael Jackson fan, huh?"

"Who isn't? He's one of the best entertainers *ever*. We used to listen to him and The Jackson 5 all the time growing up."

"You aren't old enough to know anything about The Jackson 5."

"Like I said, my parents have all their music—*The Jackson 5*, *The Jacksons* and Michael's solo albums—and I've probably downloaded most of his songs. I just wish I'd had a chance to see him in concert."

"My parents went to see The Jacksons on their Triumph Tour in 1981, and my mother still has her T-shirt. She said it was one of the best concerts she'd ever seen." They continued discussing their favorite music artists and concerts until he arrived at her house. He helped her out of the car, escorted her up the walkway and waited while she unlocked the door.

He followed her inside, and Siobhan turned to face him. "I had a good time tonight, although I'm probably going to have nightmares about somebody chasing me after seeing that movie," she added with a chuckle. "Next time, I think I'll stick to romances or something a little less creepy."

He smiled inwardly. She'd said *next time*. "Hey, there was a happy ending and some romance. He saved her from the bad guys, and don't you remember the part where the hero made love to the heroine on the beach beneath the

stars? I thought that was quite romantic." Justin moved
closer. "Black velvet night, millions of stars in the sky…a
warm breeze…" He reached out, drew her into his embrace
and let his hands roam slowly down her back and over
the curve of her hips. "The play of the moonlight on your
beautiful body," he continued while gifting her with kisses
on the shell of her ear, along her jaw and column of her
neck. "The sound of waves crashing against the shore…"
She trembled against him and gasped softly. Justin took
full advantage and slid his tongue between her parted lips.
Their tongues twined and tangled, and he angled his head
to deepen the kiss.

"Justin," Siobhan whispered against his lips.

Instead of replying, he swept her into his arms, strode
across the living room and sat on the nearest sofa with
Siobhan cradled in his lap. He continued to kiss her greed-
ily, feeding from the sweetness of her mouth. She wrapped
her arms around his neck and returned the kiss with equal
passion, surprising him and forcing a low growl from his
throat. She rocked her bottom against him, and he grew
harder with each movement. His erection throbbed, and
fire shot through his veins. Justin felt his control slipping
and tried to slow down.

Siobhan's response to him confirmed what he already
knew. At some point, they would end up sleeping together—
the chemistry between them was too strong to deny—and
when it happened, he didn't want her to have any regrets.
Somehow he found the strength to end the kiss. He eased
back, and they shared a smile. She rested her head on his
shoulder, and he let his head drop back against the sofa,
closed his eyes and waited for his galloping heart to slow.

At length, he sat up. "I'd better get going." When she
lifted her head, he couldn't resist one more kiss.

She scooted off his lap and stood.

He came to his feet and took her hand. "Walk me to

the door." Once there, he gathered her in his embrace once more. "I'll call you."

"Okay."

He placed a gentle kiss on her lips and released her. "Sleep well, baby." He opened the door and, without waiting for a response from her, sauntered down the walkway to his car.

The crisp night air did nothing to cool his insides, and neither did the thirty-minute drive to his house. What he needed was a good run, but no one went running in LA after midnight. Instead, he showered and headed for his office. Justin sat staring at the computer screen and thinking about Siobhan. Normally, he wouldn't waste time on any woman who sent out as many conflicting signals as Siobhan did, but everything about her fascinated him. And now that he'd tasted the fire beneath her icy exterior, walking away was the furthest thing from his mind.

Without thinking, Justin picked up his cell and typed: Are u asleep? The minutes ticked off while he waited for a response. When none came, he assumed Siobhan had been able to sleep after all, so he turned his attention to the list of codes on his screen. His cell buzzed, and his fingers froze on the keyboard. He unlocked the screen and read Siobhan's reply: No, can't sleep.

Why not?

Thinking about that movie…thanks to u.

Me? U agreed. But if ur afraid, I'd be more than happy to come over and protect u.

That won't be necessary. I'm a big girl & I can take care of myself.

So, when are we going out again? I'll let u pick the movie.

I don't know if that's a good idea.

Not a date, just two people having a good time. No commitments.

There was a slight delay, and then Siobhan replied: I'll let you know. Good night.

Good night.

He tossed the cell on the desk. Justin wasn't looking for a long-term relationship any more than Siobhan, but a short affair? That he could handle.

Siobhan powered off her cell, plugged it into the charger and climbed into bed. She reached up to turn off the lamp and pulled the sheet over her body. She should have ignored his text and let him think she had gone to bed. She was wide-awake, but not for the reason she'd told him. True, she had never been a big fan of thrillers, but that movie hadn't come close to stirring up the raw emotions Justin had in her. Even though he had left her house more than two hours ago, she could still feel his hands all over her body. And every time he kissed her, she lost more and more of her willpower. She shook her head. Being around Justin was dangerous to her well-being.

He made her feel things she didn't want to feel and do the things she used to enjoy—everything she had purposely put aside since Malcolm's accident. Siobhan closed her eyes to shut out the memories that refused to stay buried. Tonight they came back in full force—from her choosing to leave sixteen-year-old Brandon in charge while she went to meet her friends and arriving home to find flashing red lights and paramedics tending to a bloodied and unconscious Malcolm, to her parents' concerned and questioning gazes and Siobhan's own rising guilt. She was the oldest, and her parents had trusted her to take care of her siblings.

Tears leaked from the corners of her eyes. She had let her parents down that day, and she promised herself that it would never happen again. Of course, they hadn't blamed her, but had Siobhan been there watching her eleven-year-old baby brother, he might not have got that gash along his hairline that required twelve stitches, or the concussion.

After that incident, she'd turned to her books, graduating high school and college at the top of her class while working summers at the family company. She rarely hung out with her friends and worked hard to make her family, especially her parents, proud. She'd slipped up with Arthur, and having *fun* had cost her thousands of dollars, not to mention almost costing her the coveted PR director's position.

Now there was Justin. Siobhan didn't believe in repeating the same mistakes, but he made her feel different and she enjoyed being with him. Still, she wasn't sure she should allow him to get too close.

Chapter 7

Siobhan woke up Sunday morning feeling out of sorts and exhausted from tossing and turning all night. She'd fallen asleep thinking about Justin and his sweet kisses, and they were the first things on her mind when she woke up. Maybe a good workout would help excise him from her brain—Morgan swore exercising helped reduce stress—except her brother's gym was closed on Sundays. She could always go for a jog, but the thought of running brought a deep frown to her face. She settled on a cup of chamomile tea and some soft jazz out on her small patio.

Two hours later, she gave up all hope of relaxing and called her brother, who agreed to meet her at the gym.

Khalil unlocked the door to let Siobhan in, then locked it behind her. He kissed her cheek.

"Thanks for coming in. I hope it didn't interfere with any of your weekend plans," she said.

"No. You know I like to wake up in my own bed, *alone*."

She shook her head and followed him to the elliptical

trainers. All of her brothers loved women, but Khalil was the worst of the bunch. Women had been falling over the former model since his teenage days, but he had never been serious about one.

He leaned against the machine next to the one she climbed on and folded his arms. "Okay, sis. What's got you so tense that you're calling me to open the gym on a Sunday morning? Brandon said you'd be in next week."

Not wanting him to know the real reason for her anxiety, she said, "I've been working a lot of hours and getting ready for the launch of the new mattress. This is my first big project since taking over as PR director, and it's got me a little stressed, that's all." She set the program and started with easy strides.

Khalil flashed a dimpled smile. "Siobhan, you can write press releases and shut down publicity nightmares in your sleep, so I'll ask again—what's going on?"

Siobhan kept up her pace and rolled her eyes. "Why do you think something is going on?"

"For starters, you've never asked me to open the gym on a Sunday for an hour workout, and Brandon mentioned some new guy you were seeing."

Some days she wished she didn't have brothers. "Khalil, I can't work out if you're going to keep talking to me," she huffed.

He eyed her a moment longer, straightened, then sauntered toward the other side of the gym. "When you're done with your warm-up, come on over to the bench press," he called over his shoulder.

Two minutes in, and Siobhan's legs were already burning. It would be a miracle if she completed the entire twenty minutes. "That's what happens when I don't go to the gym for two weeks," she muttered.

When the timer went off, she slowed to a stop and sighed

in relief. If this was an indication of how her workout would be, she might as well skip the rest and go home.

"Two minutes' rest," Khalil called out.

She made a face at him and half walked, half staggered to where he stood waiting.

He laughed. "You know the drill. You can't let your muscles cool down." Khalil was one of the best personal trainers in the business, and his workouts always produced results. He glanced down at his watch. "All right. Three sets of fifteen."

Siobhan lay on the bench and adjusted her body.

"Since you haven't been here in a couple of weeks, we'll start at eighty pounds instead of your usual one hundred and work our way up. Ready?" He lifted the bar from the floor with one hand and placed it on the rack.

"Show-off." She positioned her hands on the bar.

He shrugged and gestured for her to start.

An hour later, she flopped down on a mat and groaned. "What was I thinking?" Every inch of her body ached.

Khalil lowered himself next to her and handed her an opened bottle of water.

She dragged herself to a sitting position and took the bottle. "Thanks."

"So, did that help you forget the guy?"

Siobhan paused with the bottle halfway to her mouth.

"Don't bother to deny it. This isn't the first time the gym has been open during off-hours. Just ask Brandon or Malcolm."

"Or you?"

He nodded. "What happened? Did he hurt you? Because if he did, we're not going to hold back this time."

"No, he hasn't hurt me. We've only gone out a few times, but he asked me out again and—"

"And you're trying to come up with a million and one excuses why you can't go." Khalil let out an exasperated sigh. "Look, I know what happened last time has you a little gun-shy about dating again, but you can't lock your-self in a closet or blame the next guy. You're a beautiful woman, Vonnie, and you deserve to be happy." He chuck-led and shook his head. "I can't believe I'm saying this to my sister. Brandon's gonna kill me if he finds out I said anything other than 'no guy is good enough for my sister,' so how about we keep this little conversation between us?"

Siobhan smiled. Of her three brothers, Khalil had al-ways been the most levelheaded when it came to her and Morgan dating, unless the guy did something to hurt ei-ther of them. Then he became a totally different and scary person.

He placed a hand on her shoulder. "And I know there's more to it than that. It's okay to let your guard down a little."

"I know." She said the words, but had no idea how to do that anymore.

After three days, Siobhan still hadn't recovered from her workout. She could barely lift her arms, walk or bend. Even breathing hurt. She was supposed to go back to the gym tonight, but the notion of putting her body through more torture wasn't appealing…at all. Khalil knew what Siobhan would be thinking and had sent her a reminder text earlier, cautioning her that it would only get worse if she didn't keep up with her regimen.

"Siobhan, I have the sample ad printouts from Market-ing you asked for," her secretary said, entering the office.

She reached for the folder and winced with the move-ment.

"Are you okay?"

"Yes, fine. Just did a strenuous workout, that's all."

"Oh, okay. I have everything set up in the conference room for your staff meeting."

"Thanks. I'll be there in a moment." Siobhan waited until the woman walked out before gingerly rising to her feet and following. She groaned. The worst part was that all this misery hadn't kept Justin off her mind for one second. She still wanted him—wanted him to hold her, to touch her, kiss her... Of course, it hadn't helped that he'd sent her text messages wishing her a good day every day this week. Her first thought had been to pretend she hadn't seen them, but her upbringing wouldn't allow her to ignore him. Instead, she'd sent him a cordial reply wishing him the same. She had never felt so conflicted in her life, and she still hadn't answered his question about their next date.

Pushing thoughts of Justin to the back of her mind, Siobhan entered the conference room and called the meeting to order. "Good morning, everyone. Tomorrow's the launch of our newest product, and I want to make sure we're ready to hit the market in a big way. Take a moment to go over the listing in your first handout. If you can think of any other places where we can advertise, by all means, please let me know." She inquired about each phase, from videos and photos updated on the website, to brochures being sent to hospitals and care facilities, to email, Twitter and Facebook blasts. As expected, Gordon took issue with all the "newfangled" aspects of communication.

"Television and radio have worked for the company until now, and I don't see any reason to change it."

"We're still using radio and television, but we also have to keep up with the best ways to reach our customers. Many people use social media to communicate, and if we want to compete, we'll need to do the same." She thought that would be the end of the argument, but boy, was she wrong. It turned into a full-scale debate with the other team members, and Siobhan ended up having to cancel lunch with her friends.

By the time the meeting ended, she was so angry she

had to take a walk outside for a few minutes. Otherwise, Gordon Samuels might be in need of that mattress to relieve the pressure from all the bruises he'd have after she kicked his behind. When Siobhan got back to her office, her father was waiting and stood at her entrance.

"Daddy! I didn't know you were here." She hugged him, and he kissed her cheek.

"I wanted to check on you. I heard about the meeting and Gordon."

She released a deep sigh. "He complains about everything I do and tries to undermine me at every turn. It's like he's waiting for me to make one little mistake so he can prove I can't do this job. He's said more than once that the only reason I got the job is because I'm your daughter."

He gestured her to one of the visitor chairs across from her desk and took the other one. "Siobhan, don't you worry about what Gordon or anyone else thinks. Thad and I gave you the position because you're the most qualified. I'm proud of you, baby. This was your first big project, and you've exceeded my expectations."

"Thank you, Daddy." Hearing her father say he had faith in her abilities drained her anger and brought tears to her eyes. All she ever wanted was to make him proud.

"That said, I know you've been working way more hours than necessary." He stood. "Don't forget what I told you."

She dropped her head guiltily. "I won't."

He smiled and patted her shoulder, then exited.

Siobhan rounded her desk and sat in her own chair. She retrieved her cell to call Kendra to reschedule lunch and saw she had a voice mail from Justin. Her finger hovered over the button for several seconds before she listened to the message. Just the sound of his sexy voice had her agreeing to whatever he asked.

"Hey, Siobhan. I know you've been working hard to get ready for the big project reveal this week. I know you knocked it out of the park, so how about lunch tomorrow to celebrate?"

She banged the phone softly against her temple. This was *exactly* why she should have waited until later to play the message. He always said things that made her feel all weird inside. She let out a frustrated groan and hit the re-dial button.

"Hey, Justin. I got your message," she began when his voice mail picked up, "and I… Lunch tomorrow sounds good—around twelve thirty? I know a nice place we can go." She rattled off the name and address of the restaurant and disconnected. Siobhan leaned back in the chair and closed her eyes. An image of Justin's hands and lips moving over her body filled her head. Her nipples tightened, and heat spread between her legs. Her eyes snapped open, and she sat up abruptly. "Lunch, Siobhan. That. Is. *All*," she muttered.

She dialed Kendra's number. "Hey, girl."

"You sound worn-out," Kendra said.

"If you had to sit in a meeting with that idiot Gordon for almost three hours, you'd be worn-out, too."

She laughed. "Well, at least you have Justin to make you feel better."

Siobhan groaned.

"What? Did you kick him to the curb already?"

"No, but—"

"But you want to."

"I didn't say that."

"True, but I know you."

"I'm not planning to *kick him to the curb*."

"Fine—if you're not, prove it."

"What do you mean?"

"Bring him to my anniversary party on Friday."

"Kendra," Siobhan started, but Kendra cut her off.

"You said he's a nice guy, and you're not trying to dump him, so bring him. Gotta go. I'll expect you both. 'Bye."

Siobhan heard the beep signaling the end of the call and sighed. Though she wanted to keep Justin at a distance, she couldn't deny yearning to spend more time with him.

Justin had made good progress this morning getting the temperature sensors to work properly. He woke up energized and wondered if his approaching lunch date with Siobhan had anything to do with it. She had surprised him by agreeing so readily. He glanced up at the clock on his laptop—three hours to go, so she still had time to cancel. Chuckling, he went back to typing.

A while later his cell rang. He fully expected to see Siobhan's name on the display, but blew out a sigh of relief upon seeing Bobby's name.

"What's up, Bobby?" Justin said when he answered.

Bobby laughed. "That's what I want to know about you. I'm calling to see how the system is going."

"It's going. Still having some trouble with the temperature sensor portion."

"Do you think you'll be ready by the time you meet with Gray?"

"I sure as hell hope so. Every time I think I've got the problem solved, something else messes up. How's your grandfather?"

"Ornery as ever. The doctor keeps telling him to take it easy, but the old man can't seem to stay away from the winery. I spend more time shuttling him back and forth to the house than taking care of the business."

"It has to be hard not being able to have a hands-on presence in the business you started from the ground up."

"Yeah, I know. I'd probably be the same way."

"Why don't you offer him a compromise, maybe let him spend two or three hours at the winery a couple of days a week? I'm sure you can have a comfortable lounger placed in the office and get a mobile work surface."

"I don't know why I didn't think of that. You wouldn't happen to be available to fly down today and design a work space, would you?"

Justin laughed. "Sorry, bro. I'm meeting someone for lunch and I can't cancel, but I'll be happy to email you some recommendations."

"Another prospective company?"

"No. A lunch date."

"I didn't know you were seeing someone."

"It's nothing serious. I'm not looking to settle down, and neither is she."

"Are you sure? How old is she?"

His brows knit together. "I have no idea. I'm guessing somewhere around thirty."

"Man, women who've passed that thirty mark *are* looking for marriage—I don't care what they say. If you're not planning to stick around for the long haul, I suggest you make that crystal clear, otherwise you're going to find yourself in the same situation you were in before."

That was true for Justin's ex, but Siobhan gave him the impression that she meant precisely what she'd said—no relationships. "I don't think so. She was pretty adamant." He peeked at his watch. "I have to go. I'll try to send you the work-surface information tonight or tomorrow."

"Thanks, and enjoy your lunch."

"I plan to." He disconnected, changed clothes and left for his date.

Justin kept telling himself that he and Siobhan were on the same page—no long-term commitments and no emotional entanglements. However, he hadn't bargained for the rapid pace of his heartbeat and the excitement flowing through him, not to mention the overwhelming need to kiss her, when he saw her walk through the restaurant door.

And when she smiled at him, a crazy sensation started in the middle of his chest.

"Hey." Siobhan leaned up and kissed him. "You okay? You looked like you were deep in thought."

He pushed the feelings aside and smiled. "I'm fine."

"Did you have any problems finding the place?"

"Not at all. I already got our table." They followed the hostess to a booth, and she handed them menus. "How did your project go?" he asked.

Her eyes sparkled, and she gave him a brilliant smile. "Great. It was my first big one, and my boss is pleased."

"Congratulations." He studied her over his menu. He'd never seen her so animated and relaxed, and he liked it. The passion in her voice and the warmth in her smile enthralled him even more. "Do you have to go back to work this afternoon?"

She lifted her eyes from the menu. "Yes. Why?"

Justin shrugged. "I figured we could play hooky and really celebrate."

"It sounds like fun, but I can't."

The wistful note in her tone gave him pause. "That's okay. We can save it for another time." After they placed their orders, he asked, "What exactly do you do at your job?"

"Public relations, marketing, that kind of stuff. What about you? You never mentioned where you work."

"Actually, I did. The night we met, I told you I like working for myself," he added when she gave him a questioning look. "I design programs from the comfort of my home."

"Oh, yes. I remember. Your programs must have done well if you're able to afford to work from home."

He recognized her ploy to gain more information about him and hesitated over how much information to share. Though he didn't think she fell into the same category as the women who assumed he had millions stashed away, Justin decided to play it safe. "They do well enough to keep the lights on."

She nodded, and the conversation turned to growing up. Over their food, they shared stories about favorite classes and teachers in school. Eventually he saw Siobhan look at her watch. "Time for you to head back?"

"Unfortunately, yes."

He held up the dessert menus left by the waitress. "You want to get dessert to go?"

"No, thank you. Um, I know it's short notice, but my friend is having an anniversary party tomorrow night. Would you like to go with me?"

"Of course." Attending the party would give him more time to spend with her. "How long have they been married?"

"Only two years, but they never had a reception, so they're doing it big this year." She gave him the particulars and agreed upon a time for him to pick her up.

After paying the bill, he walked her to her car. "I'm glad your project turned out well." He lowered his head and kissed her, then remembered that they were standing on a public street and grudgingly released her.

"I…I'd better go," Siobhan said breathlessly.

He nodded and waited for her to drive off, and then went back to his car. He took a deep breath and exhaled slowly. He liked kissing her too damn much, and there were other emotions trying to creep into the mix, ones he didn't want to accept.

So much for *casual fun*.

"Thank you for coming with me tonight, Justin," Siobhan said as he escorted her into the elegantly decorated hotel ballroom where the party was being held.

"Thank you for asking. I'm glad I can spend more time with you."

So was she, but she didn't say so.

"You made it," Kendra said, approaching them and reaching out to hug Siobhan.

She handed Kendra a gift bag. "Happy anniversary. Where's Doug?"

"He's somewhere mingling." Kendra turned to Justin. "It's good to see you again, Justin."

"Same here. Happy anniversary." Justin handed her an envelope.

"Wow. Thank you. I think Cynthia saved a couple of seats for you guys at her table. Dinner will be served in a few. Then we can get to the real fun. Oh, there's Doug. Let me go see what he wants." She waved back and hurried off.

"That was very nice of you," Siobhan said to Justin.

He shrugged. "I was raised not to go anywhere empty-handed."

She'd never met a more thoughtful man. "Let's get our seats." They joined Cynthia, her husband, Garrett, and two other couples at the table, and kept up a steady stream of conversation throughout dinner.

Afterward, Kendra and Doug cut the cake and shared a dance, then invited everyone to join them.

Justin extended his hand and led Siobhan out to the dance floor. "I've been waiting for an opportunity to dance with you again."

"Is that right?"

"Yes. I enjoyed it the last time."

"So did I."

He smiled, tightened his arms around her and placed a kiss behind her ear. Feeling his lips on her skin and his body grinding lightly against hers sent shock waves through her system. He rested his cheek against her temple and hummed along with the slow ballad. She melted into him, and a feeling of contentment washed over her. When the song ended, he released her and she stepped back.

"Can I get you something to drink?"

"Yes, please. A glass of white wine would be nice."

He led her back to their table and went over to the open bar set up across the room.

Cynthia smiled. "Well, well."

"Not one word, Cyn," Siobhan said, turning her head to hide her own smile.

"What?" Cynthia asked innocently.

Facing her friend again, she said, "This is really nice. Kendra's parents did a fabulous job."

"Uh-huh, it's nice. And so is seeing you and Justin together."

Before she could comment, Justin returned with two glasses of wine.

"Here you go, sweetheart."

"Thank you."

Their eyes held as they sipped, and she felt something pass between them. He lifted her hand and placed a kiss on the back. Out of her periphery, Siobhan saw Cynthia grinning and fanning herself.

"Now, that's what I'm talking about," Cynthia said sotto voce, lifting her own glass.

Siobhan didn't comment.

"Dance with me," Justin said when another ballad came on.

Siobhan followed him back out to the dance floor and wrapped her arms around his neck.

"I'm glad they're playing a lot of slow songs because I like holding you in my arms."

"I like it, too."

A slow grin curved Justin's lips. "Then we'll need to do it more often." He touched his mouth to hers. "Every chance we get," he whispered.

They danced through every slow song that played, and by the time he took her home, her body and mind were in a jumble.

"Thank you, again, for coming to the party with me," she said as they stood in her entryway.

"I enjoyed myself."

She leaned up, intending to give him a quick kiss, but as soon as their lips touched and he swept his hot tongue into her mouth, all rational thoughts went out the window. Justin deepened the kiss, thoroughly exploring every inch of her mouth.

He broke off the kiss and rested his forehead against hers. "I'd better leave while I still can."

Siobhan nodded, though she wasn't sure she really wanted him to leave. He kissed her once more and slipped out the door.

She closed her eyes and leaned against it, her breathing still ragged. She hadn't planned on meeting a man like him and didn't know how long she would be able to keep her guard up.

Chapter 8

Justin increased his pace on the park's running trail and found a steady rhythm. Two days. It had been two days since he'd seen Siobhan and shared a kiss that he hadn't been able to shake from his mind. He'd kissed her several times before, but he hadn't been prepared for the sensations that engulfed him during that last one. He had avoided calling her since the party on Friday evening because he needed to think about what it meant. Common sense told him now would be a good time to cut his losses, but the degree to which he wanted her almost guaranteed that he'd ignore that little piece of wisdom.

He slowed to a jog and eventually a walk, then started in the direction of his car. When Justin got home, he showered and, against his better judgment, called Siobhan and asked if he could stop by her house for a few minutes. She replied with a simple "Yes."

Forty-five minutes later, he pulled up to her house, hopped out of the car and strode up to her door.

Siobhan opened the door, concern creasing her brow. "Justin, is everything okay?"

"It is now," he answered, backing her into the house, kicking the door shut and hauling her into his arms. He brought his mouth crashing down on hers. She matched him stroke for stroke as he intensified the connection and indulged in a craving he felt might never be satisfied.

When they finally came up for air, they were both breathing heavily. One look in her beautiful brown eyes, and Justin couldn't resist one more taste of her luscious lips, taking his time and twining his tongue lazily with hers as if he had all the time in the world. "I could hold you and kiss you all night," he murmured between kisses. She ran her hands over his abs and chest then around his neck, and stroked his nape lightly. He shuddered. Justin's hands made a slow path down her back, and lower still to cup her buttocks, bringing her flush against his arousal. He wanted her to feel what she was doing to him.

Siobhan gasped, broke off the kiss and slumped against him. She trembled, and he tightened his arms around her. They stood this way for who knew how long before she backed out of his hold.

"Do you want something to eat or drink?" she asked.

"Nah, I'm good. But thanks. I should probably get going. I have some work to do." And he needed to get away from her, or else they'd be naked and in her bed within the blink of an eye.

"You came all the way over here just to...?"

"Kiss you?"

She nodded.

"Yeah. Those lips have been calling me since I left you on Friday. And if I stand here one more minute, I'll be doing more than just kissing you."

She laughed nervously. "Then I guess you should get going."

Justin kissed her softly. "I'll see you later, sweetheart." With great effort, he placed one foot in front of the other until he was in his car. Seeing Siobhan standing in the doorway tempted him to go back inside and finish what he'd started. He stayed parked there until she closed the door.

All the way home, he questioned his impulsivity. Never had he felt so out of control with a woman. And what the hell had got into him, driving across town for the sole purpose of kissing one? He was no closer to an answer by the time he reached his house. He went straight to his office to work on his program. The meeting with Mr. Gray was a week away, and he wasn't close to being ready. Once again, he had allowed his focus to shift. Justin shook his head and tried to concentrate, but gave up after an hour and decided to find and send Bobby the information he had promised.

As soon as he got back into his work, the phone rang. He groaned and snatched up the receiver.

"Hey, big brother," Jocelyn said in her usually bubbly voice when he answered.

"What's up, Short Stack? If you're calling to continue last week's conversation, I have to go."

She laughed. "No, I'm not calling to mess with you. We got our grades back from the engineering project. We got an A."

"Congratulations! I'm so proud of you. Did you call Mom and Dad?"

"Not yet. I wanted to tell you first since you helped us. I'm so glad you're my brother."

"And I'm glad you're my sister, even though you can be a pain in the neck sometimes."

"I don't know what you mean," Jocelyn said, feigning innocence.

"Right. So I guess you've forgotten all about that double-team last week."

"I wasn't going to say anything, but since you brought it up, are you any closer to me getting a sister-in-law?"

"It's definitely time to hang up now. Don't you need to make another call or something?"

"Ha-ha. I can take a hint. Keep me posted. Love you, Justin."

"Love you, too, Joce," Justin said, hanging up. *Sister-in-law.* He shook his head. Granted, he liked Siobhan and enjoyed being with her, but he wasn't thinking about or ready for anything so serious as marriage. But the thought of settling down didn't make him break out in hives, either.

Justin made some headway on his system, but Siobhan was never far from his mind. Since meeting her, he'd got back the spark he used to have before his grandfather died—the spontaneity and enjoyment of living, instead of the monotony of working day in and day out. She was intelligent, driven, beautiful, and despite her reserved appearance, his gut told him that underneath she possessed the same adventurous spirit as him.

And he wanted nothing more than to unleash all that passion she kept locked inside.

"Good morning, beautiful. I hope your Monday is off to a good start."

Siobhan's eyes slid closed briefly upon hearing Justin's smooth-as-silk greeting. She had contemplated not answering, but the temptation to hear his voice was too hard to resist. "Good morning, yourself. I hit the ground running. What about you?"

Justin laughed. "I hit the ground running, *literally.* I just got back from my daily jog. Maybe you'll join me one day."

She snorted. "Please. I hate running, so that is one activity you'll be doing on your own."

"Hmm. Then maybe I can tempt you into trying some other activities."

"Oh?" She was already beyond tempted to engage in some *other* activities, activities that included them naked in her bed or his.

"I can think of a few off the top of my head, like dancing, a walk on the beach—or finishing what we started on Sunday," he added huskily. "What do you say? We can do any one or all three of them."

Yes, yes, yes! the spontaneous, fun-loving woman inside her shouted. But her practical self reminded her what had happened the last time. "This week is going to be a long one for me, and I just had another project dropped in my lap."

"No problem. Whenever you have some time."

She heard the disappointment in his voice and added, "I'm sure we can figure something out, but I'd better get back to work."

"All right. I'll be thinking about you, and try not to work too hard, Siobhan."

"I'll try. And, Justin?"

"Yeah, baby."

"Thanks for calling." She disconnected, turned her cell off and dropped it in her purse.

She placed a calming hand on her belly and drew in a deep breath. Her feelings for Justin intensified each time they spoke, and she finally realized what made him such a risk. He made her do the one thing she feared most— lose control.

In an effort to stop her growing attraction, she shut down and immersed herself in work, like she always did when she became overwhelmed. She didn't bother to stop for lunch and stayed way past normal business hours. By the time she trudged to her car, the cleaning crew had come and gone, and hers was one of four vehicles left in the underground parking garage. She waved to the security guard and slid behind the wheel.

"At least there's no traffic this time of night," she mumbled. Without the usual crowded freeway, Siobhan made it home in less than half an hour.

After consuming shrimp stir-fry for dinner, she showered and climbed into bed. As soon as she closed her eyes, Justin's handsome face appeared in her mind, and memories of their heated kisses in her entryway awakened her desires once more. She wanted to call him, ask him to come over and put out the flame he'd started. But doing that would be akin to opening Pandora's box again, and she had worked diligently over the past two years to keep it closed. No way would she survive another fiasco like Arthur.

They'd met at a restaurant near her office three years ago. Both had been waiting for lunch partners and struck up a conversation. After seeing each other at the same spot two more times, he'd said it was fate and asked her to lunch. Though it had taken weeks, Arthur finally won Siobhan over with his infectious smile and charming personality. It didn't hurt that he was easy on the eyes.

Now there was Justin. And everything she'd felt for Arthur paled in comparison to the emotions Justin aroused in her.

Groaning, she flipped over onto her stomach and put the pillow over her head to drown out her thoughts. It didn't help. She tossed and turned for a good hour before giving up all hope of going to sleep, and decided to get up and do some work.

Siobhan repeated this cycle for the next two nights. During the day, her mask stayed firmly in place. She smiled and conducted business as usual, and no one suspected her inner turmoil.

Thursday evening she sat at her desk massaging the

muscles in her neck. She'd kept up with her workouts, and after a couple of days the soreness typically subsided. But this time her muscles still ached. She leaned back in the chair, closed her eyes and rubbed her temples. The headache that had started earlier was intensifying, and a wave of nausea washed over her. Siobhan knew she probably should have eaten something, but the thought of food held no appeal. Her cell rang, and she prayed it wasn't Brandon or, worse, one of her parents. She felt a measure of relief when she saw Justin's name on the display.

"Hi, Justin," she said.

"Hey, Siobhan. I'm just checking on you. Hope your week hasn't been too bad."

Why was he always so thoughtful? It was one more reason she had such a hard time remaining firm in her decision to stop seeing him. "Wish I could say it's been a piece of cake, but I'd be lying. I'm still at the office."

There was a pause. Then he said, "Siobhan, it's ten o'clock. That's kind of late. Is anyone else there with you?"

"No, but—"

"You're there alone this time of night?" he asked, his voice rising. "I understand you have a lot to do, but can't you take it home? I don't like the idea of you being in your office alone. Do you want me to come keep you company? I promise not to distract you in any way, but I just want to be sure you're safe."

"I appreciate your offer, Justin, but I'm leaving soon. I'll be gone before you get here." And she didn't want him to know where she worked, especially since she'd never told him her real last name.

"Have you stayed this late all week?"

"Yes," she answered guiltily. The word tumbled out before she had a chance to lie.

She heard his frustrated sigh. "Sweetheart, you're going

to burn out if you keep this up. I bet you haven't eaten, either."

Siobhan didn't answer.

"Just as I thought. And there's no way you can concentrate on an empty stomach. Go home, baby," Justin said softly. "You need some rest."

His soft plea melted her heart. "I'm going."

"Thank you. Please call me to let me know you arrived safely."

"Okay." She hung up and held the phone against her chest. "What is he doing to me?" she whispered.

"Why are you still sitting behind that desk?"

She jumped and whirled around in her chair upon hearing the angry voice of her brother. "You scared the hell out of me, Brandon!"

"Better me than someone else," he said with a heavy scowl lining his face.

"What are you doing here?" He'd obviously come from home because, instead of the suit he'd had on during the day, he wore a pair of sweats and a T-shirt.

"That's what I came to find out about you. Mr. Daily called because he was concerned about you being here by yourself so late." Mr. Daily was the night guard in the garage.

"There's a lot to do and—"

Brandon held up a hand. "Vonnie, don't start. There's no reason for you to be here this late, and for four days straight. Yeah, he mentioned that part, too." He came around to her side of the desk, propped a hip on the end and folded his arms. "What's going on, sis? I know something's bothering you."

Siobhan smiled and waved him off. "I just want to keep on top of things, and I'm getting the second round of press releases ready."

"I've known you just about all of your life, so I'm pretty

good at figuring out when you're lying. And you are lying. You don't think I've noticed you withdrawing into yourself? You're wound so tight, I'm surprised you haven't snapped."

She came to her feet swiftly and started packing up her belongings, not wanting him to see how close he was to the truth. "You worry too much. I'm fine, really. And didn't you say I needed to go home? I can't leave if you stand here talking to me all night."

He gave her a penetrating stare and then straightened from the desk. He waited until she was done and followed her out and down to her car. "I'll be by your desk tomorrow at four forty-five, and you're leaving."

She opened her mouth to argue, but one look from her brother and she closed it.

Brandon leaned down and kissed her temple. "I'll be right behind you," he said as he shut the car door.

At this point, Siobhan didn't have the strength to argue and pulled off, fussing about overprotective brothers the entire drive. At her house, Brandon got out of his car and she started to protest, but stopped when she saw the bag in his hand.

"I figured you hadn't eaten, so I brought you some of the chicken soup I made."

This time a real smile bloomed on her face. "Thanks, Brandon. I take back everything I said about you."

He gave her a puzzled look. "I don't recall you saying anything."

"That's because you weren't in the car with me."

He laughed and gestured with his head toward the house. "Lock up."

"I will. Good night." She glanced back at him after she opened the door, and he waved her in. Closing and locking the door, she shuffled to the kitchen, dropped the tote and her purse in a kitchen chair and set the bag with her soup on the counter.

The delicious smell wafted across her nose as soon as she removed the container from the bag, and her stomach growled. She shook her head thinking about Brandon while eating. All her brothers, and father, watched over and protected her and Morgan. After every family gathering, at least one followed them home, and they never left until she and her sister had closed the door. She noticed similar qualities in Justin and realized he would probably fit in well with her family.

Justin. "Oh, shoot." She was supposed to call Justin to let him know she'd arrived home. She reached over, fished her cell out of her purse and pushed the redial button.

"I was just about to drive over," Justin said by way of greeting.

"Sorry—I was talking to my brother. I'm home now, so you don't need to come over." *Although, if he does, I might sleep better tonight...*

"Maybe you should talk to your boss. I understand having to do overtime hours, but there's no reason you should be working this late so often. And I bet he or she is at home relaxing."

Technically, *she* was the boss. "It's not that bad, and my boss doesn't require all the overtime. I just like to keep ahead of the game."

"When do you relax? I mean, you're working on the weekends when I call and late during the week."

"I do relax."

"I hope so. I won't hold you because I know you're going to be up and in your office early. Promise me you'll leave at least close to regular time tomorrow."

"I promise." Not as if she'd have much choice since Brandon was determined to camp out until she left or drag her out, if necessary.

"Good night, sweet lady. Sleep well."

"You, too." The endearment seeped into the cracks of the wall around her heart. Picking up her spoon, Siobhan finished her soup and prepared for bed.

She sat in her office the next morning feeling a little better. Her headache had subsided, and for the first time all week, she had slept five hours. Talking to Justin had been the only thing she had done differently from the other nights. His voice had a way of soothing her and…

That *couldn't* be why. Refusing to travel any further down this line of reasoning, she spun around in her chair and snatched up a document.

True to his word, Brandon appeared in her office doorway at exactly four forty-five. Siobhan had already packed up in anticipation. She stood and rounded her desk. *"Happy?"*

"Yep. Let's go. Mom call you about dinner on Sunday?" he asked as they left.

"No. When did she call you?"

"About an hour ago."

Her cell rang. They looked at each other and laughed. "Hi, Mom."

"Hi, honey. What's so funny?"

"Brandon was just asking if you'd called, and the phone rang."

"Oh. Well, you know I'm making my rounds. I assume you're coming early, as always. Any chance you'll be bringing a date?"

"Um…no, but I'll be there early."

Her mother sighed. "One of these days, I'm going to get a yes from you or one of your siblings."

"See you on Sunday, Mom." Siobhan hurried to end the call and met Brandon's smiling face.

"She wanted to know if you were bringing a date, too?"

She nodded. "I thought you were dating someone."

"Correction—I'm seeing someone *loosely.* No way am

I bringing her to a family dinner. I don't want her getting any ideas."

"That's a shame. If a guy said he was dating Morgan or me *loosely*, you, Khalil and Malcolm would have a heart attack and try to kill the guy. She could be someone's sister, too."

"Hey, I told her up front I wasn't in the market for anything serious. She said she wasn't, either, so it was her choice to proceed. What about you? Are you still seeing that guy?"

"Loosely," she answered with a laugh and opened her car door. "See you on Sunday."

He kissed her cheek. "Drive safe."

Before she could pull out of the lot, her cell rang again. "Hey, Justin."

"Hey. I want to make sure you're not staying late tonight, and if you are, to let you know that I'm coming to hang out with you."

"You'll be happy to know that I am in my car and getting ready to pull out of the lot."

"Yep, I'm happy. I'd be happier if we could have dinner together tonight, but you need to rest."

"It has been a long week." *In more ways than one.*

"I'm going to hang up because I don't want you driving while on the phone. I'll talk to you tomorrow."

Siobhan couldn't stop the smile that spread across her lips. Justin was different from the men she had gone out with in the past. They were either intimidated by her direct speech or bent over backward to try to please her, thinking it would get them on the fast track to her family's wealth. Most times, she could figure out which category they fit into within a few moments of conversation. But she couldn't get a read on Justin. He didn't seem put off by her candor at all, and that piqued her curiosity.

Siobhan jerked upright in her bed at the sound of the doorbell. She glanced over at the clock and muttered, "It

is eight o'clock on a Saturday morning." The only people
who showed up at her place this early were her brothers.
Siobhan knew it wasn't her sister because Morgan was not
a morning person. She staggered sleepily to the front door
and snatched it open.

"One of you big heads had better have a good reason to
be ringing my doorbell at this—" The rest of her rant died
in her throat when she saw Justin leaning against the column with that knee-weakening smile, and looking down-
right mouthwatering in a pair of jeans and a navy T-shirt
that outlined every muscle in his upper body.

She wanted to strangle him.

Chapter 9

"Good morning, sunshine," Justin said, his smile widening. His gaze slid lazily down her body and back up.

His frank appraisal reminded Siobhan that she had come to the door wearing a skimpy tank top and too-short shorts, her normal sleeping attire. She took a step behind the door. "What are you doing here so early?"

"I came to kidnap you."

"*Excuse* me?"

He repeated himself. "Don't worry—being kidnapped isn't always a bad thing."

She scraped a hand over her hair. Was he serious? "I don't see how being kidnapped is a good thing."

His voice dropped an octave. "That's because you've never been kidnapped by me."

Oh, Lord!

"You've been working hard all week, and I want to give you a chance to relax. What do you say, beautiful?"

With him standing there looking so good, saying no

was the furthest thing from her mind. She opened the door wider to let him in. "Okay. Give me thirty minutes to get ready."

"Take your time, and don't worry about breakfast. It's the first thing on the list this morning."

"First thing? Justin Cartwright, what are you planning?"

He grinned. "It's a surprise. We're turning off our cell phones and we're gonna have fun, *big* fun." She stood there staring at him and trying to guess what he had up his sleeve.

"Weren't you going to get dressed?"

Siobhan backed away slowly, turned around and headed down the hallway. She showered quickly and went through her closet trying to find something to wear. While searching, she questioned her sanity. She did not do *spontaneous*. And turning off her cell phone… She planned everything down to the minute. So why didn't she tell him she wasn't going unless he gave her the day's itinerary? And how long did he plan on them being gone? Siobhan inhaled deeply and resumed her search. She could do this. She assumed something casual would work since he had on jeans. It was the middle of April, but the temperatures had been unseasonably warm, near eighty degrees. She slid into a pair of black jeans and a short-sleeved faux wrap black-and-white-print top. Siobhan chose a pair of comfortable walking shoes that were still cute.

Justin stood when she entered the living room. "You look great."

"Thanks. Is this okay? Since I have no idea what you've planned, I wasn't sure what to wear."

"It's perfect, but I have something in mind a little later that might require a change of clothes. It doesn't have to be too dressy, just business casual."

She placed her hands on her hips. "I don't know if I like

this, especially not having my phone." She wasn't used to giving up control and felt a moment of panic.

He closed the distance between them and kissed her. "I didn't say not to bring it, just to turn it off for a while, and I'll do the same. I want you to enjoy yourself today, and for us to spend some uninterrupted time together. But if you feel uneasy at any time while we're out, just let me know and we'll come back."

Their gazes held as Siobhan debated what to do. Finally, she nodded. What could it hurt to have a little fun for a few hours? "I'll be right back." She went to pack a small bag, which, her being a woman, included two changes of clothes, makeup and toiletries in case she needed to freshen up.

"Ready?" Justin asked when she returned.

"Yes." She said the word, but not being in the driver's seat had butterflies fluttering in her stomach. Justin drove them to a nearby restaurant, and after they'd ordered and received their food, Siobhan began to feel antsy. "So, what's next?"

He smiled with amusement. "We're not even done with breakfast yet. You hate not being in control of everything, don't you?"

"That's not true—I just like knowing where I'm going."

He laughed. "Siobhan, I've learned something about you in these last few weeks. You have a need to control every circumstance around you, and when that doesn't happen, it makes you feel uncomfortable."

She sat stunned. In a matter of seconds, he'd uncovered her innermost feelings.

Justin grasped her hand. "I'm not asking you to change who you are, baby, but it's okay to loosen the reins a little every now and again."

Siobhan had existed this way for so long, she wasn't sure if she even knew *how* to let go.

He must have sensed her turmoil because he said, "I thought we'd go to the Santa Monica Pier for a while."

She smiled. "Thank you. I guess that's about all I'm going to get in the way of today's schedule, huh?"

Justin shrugged. "Can't give away all my secrets, but rest assured I plan to show you a good time."

"I can deal with that." They finished their meals while conversing softly.

On the way to the pier, Siobhan relaxed and watched the passing scenery. A smile curved her lips. Kendra and Cynthia would probably pass out when she told them she had gone on an *unplanned* date. It was still early when they arrived, and the amusement park and most of the shops didn't open until eleven.

"Let's go for a walk. You might want to bring your jacket, in case you get cold."

She slipped into the jacket with Justin's help, and they strolled down the path at a leisurely pace, eventually ending on the beach.

He pulled her to stand in front of him and wrapped his arms around her middle. "I don't think I planned this right."

She angled her head to look up at him. "What do you mean?"

A wolfish grin appeared on his face. "We should've come at night."

Siobhan whipped her head back around toward the water without commenting. A slow heat started between her legs when she remembered what he'd said—and *done*—after their movie date.

"What do you think?"

"I think you're outrageous."

Justin nuzzled her neck and chuckled. "So, no sex on the beach?"

"No."

"You sure? I can promise you an incredible experience."

His hot words nearly turned Siobhan's legs to molten lava. And she had no doubt he could back it up. "How do you know it'll be incredible?" she challenged. "Have you done it before?"

"I've never done it, never even thought about it until I met you. And it can only be incredible with an extraordinary and beautiful woman like you."

Just like that, her wall dropped two notches. "I think I'd like a little more privacy."

"Anywhere you want it."

They stood watching the waves awhile longer, each lost in thought.

"I see the carousel is open now. Want to ride?"

"Can't come to the pier and not ride the carousel," she said with a smile.

"Do you want to sit on one of the benches?" Justin asked when it was their turn to ride.

"I don't think so. You have to ride the horse, Justin."

He viewed the wooden horses and other animals with distrust. "How about I stand next to you to make sure you don't fall off?"

"Okay." He helped her up, and the ride started. She was transported back in time to when her family came to the pier every summer. With each revolution, her stress level diminished, and two rides later, Siobhan was having so much fun, she completely forgot about time. The temperatures warmed, so she took off her jacket and tied it around her waist. They continued the fun at the amusement park with the roller coaster, tower ride and Ferris wheel. And she ate a funnel cake, reliving another moment from her childhood.

"I've worked up an appetite with all these rides."

She laughed. "Men are always hungry." She realized the unintentional double entendre the moment it left her mouth, and Justin's smile confirmed it. Siobhan playfully socked him on the shoulder. "That's not what I meant, and you know it."

"I didn't say a word." He mimicked zipping his lips.

"You didn't have to. That smile said it all."

Justin tried to keep a straight face but couldn't, and laughter spilled from his lips. "Come on." They had a quick bite, and then he checked his watch. "We need to get going."

She really wanted to ask where, but since she was trying to adopt a go-with-the-flow type of attitude today, she swallowed the question.

In the car, he adjusted the airflow. "Make yourself comfortable. It's going to be a while before we get to our next stop."

Siobhan stared at him curiously as he wove through the traffic. Moments later, Michael Jackson's "Billie Jean" came through the speakers. She smiled over at him and settled more comfortably in the Audi's leather seat. She must have dozed off because the next she knew they were crossing the California-Nevada state line. "Vegas?"

"Yep. You said you wanted to go again." A short time later, he pulled into the Mandalay Bay Resort parking lot. "It's a quarter to six now, and we have just enough time to check in and change."

Check in? He planned for them to stay overnight? In the same room?

"Siobhan?"

His voice shattered her reverie. "Huh? Oh." He stood at her open door with his hand extended. He helped her out of the car, and she reached back inside to grab her jacket while he removed their bags from the trunk. It didn't take long to check in, and she was left speechless by the suite's elegance—king-size bed, living room and a wall of windows overlooking the Strip. The bathroom had double sinks, a large glass shower and a soaking tub large enough for two. Siobhan startled slightly when Justin came up behind her.

"Is this okay?"

"It's beautiful, but I didn't expect to be gone overnight or the whole weekend."

"I booked the room for one night, and like I told you earlier, I'll take you back whenever you're ready."

This suite wasn't cheap, but he was willing to lose his money for her comfort. There went another notch. "No, it's fine." She didn't want him to waste his money, she rationalized.

"You can change first."

She nodded, picked up her bag and went into the bathroom. Emotions bubbled up within her, and she braced her hands on the sink and bowed her head. This man made it almost impossible to remain unmoved.

As soon as he heard the shower running, Justin made a quick trip downstairs to pick up tickets for the show. He rushed back upstairs, stretched out on the bed and waited for Siobhan to change. He couldn't believe the transformation. The straitlaced, restrained businesswoman whom he'd met that first night—and just about every time they'd gone out—had been replaced with a fun-loving siren who turned him on even more. He still sensed some hesitancy on her part, however, and he wanted to do everything in his power to give her a weekend she would never forget.

"Your turn."

He sat up at the sound of her voice and did a slow appraisal. She wore a pair of white slacks, a green top and matching low-heeled green pumps. She had applied minimal makeup that accentuated her light brown eyes and had slicked her ear-length curly hair back on one side. Justin slowly rose from the bed and approached her. He kissed her cheek, being careful not to smudge her makeup. "You are absolutely gorgeous."

"Thank you."

"I'll be right back." Justin smiled the whole time while showering and dressing. Fifteen minutes later, he emerged from the bathroom.

"Don't you look handsome," Siobhan said, sauntering his way and draping her arms around his neck.

"What, this old outfit?" he teased, glancing down at the black slacks and pale purple dress shirt.

She laughed. "I'm really enjoying this trip. So, where to next?"

"Ah, so you're finally getting the hang of this fun stuff. See, I told you being kidnapped isn't so bad."

"Nope. I might have to let you kidnap me more often."

"Don't tempt me, woman. Keep talking like that and I may never let you go." Where had that come from?

Her eyebrows shot up, and he heard her sharp intake of breath.

The atmosphere went from playful to serious in an instant. "We should get going." They took the elevator down and walked through the casino, passing various shops. Several other people were headed in the same direction. Justin stopped. "You said you missed out on a show the last time you came to Vegas, and I know how much you like Michael Jackson, so I figured this would be the best of both worlds." He handed her the tickets.

Siobhan's eyes lit up and she let out a squeal. "*Oh. My. God!* I can't believe it."

She threw her arms around his neck and gave him a kiss that left him gasping for breath and drew the attention of some passersby.

One older man chuckled and said, "Your wife must love Michael Jackson."

Not bothering to correct the assumption, Justin said, "She does."

Siobhan was too excited to notice and grabbed Justin's hand, tugging him in the direction of the theater. "Where are we sitting?"

"You have the tickets."

She giggled and waved them in the air. "Oh, yeah." She studied the tickets and then whipped her head around. "Row D?"

He nodded and laughed.

Once they reached their seats and she realized they were in the center section, she did a little shimmy in her seat. "This is *fantastic*. I still can't believe it." She reached up and cupped his jaw. "Thank you, Justin. I will never, ever forget this night."

Those strange emotions surfaced again. "You're welcome."

He was falling for this woman and wasn't sure whether a casual, no-strings-attached relationship was really what he wanted anymore.

Siobhan bounced in her seat, waiting for the show to begin. Their seats were in the fourth row, so close that she could see everything. Moments later the lights went down and the music began. Between the aerial performances, acrobatics and amazing dance choreography going on simultaneously, she didn't know where to settle her gaze first. She and Justin clapped and sang along to their favorite songs, and were held spellbound by a woman on a rope, hanging from the ceiling dancing to "Dirty Diana." Siobhan leaned over and whispered, "She has phenomenal body strength."

Justin chuckled.

The highlight of the performance, in her mind, had to be the hologram of Michael performing on the stage with the dancers. They performed so precisely, she would have sworn Michael was on the stage for real.

Siobhan was still humming and smiling after the show, and Justin bought her a T-shirt for a souvenir. "I don't know if I want to wear it or frame it."

"I can solve that problem. Stay right here." He disappeared in the crowd and came back minutes later with a second shirt. "Now one to frame and one to wear."

"I can't let you do this. You already bought one." She opened her purse, and he put a hand on her arm.

"This weekend is my treat, sweetheart. Now dinner."

"Dare I ask where?"

"You can ask…"

She tilted her chin and strutted past him. "That's okay. I don't need to know. I'm fine."

Justin shook his head and laughed. "You're learning."

They walked clear across the other side of the resort and ended up at the House of Blues. This night kept getting better and better. She ordered a shrimp po'boy with French fries and a margarita, while he opted for jambalaya and a Long Island Iced Tea. With the way she had eaten today, Siobhan would need to hit the gym every day next week to work it all off, but she didn't regret one second. Over dinner, they discussed their favorite parts of the show and what they wished had been included. This had been the best date she'd ever had, and she was a little sad that it would be over tomorrow. And she hadn't even thought about turning on her cell phone once. "What's next?" she asked eagerly.

Justin took a sip of his drink before responding. "You decide."

She brought her hand to her heart. "What? I get to be in control?" she said teasingly.

A wide grin split his face. "I'm quite content to share every once in a while."

"All right, then. Let's go to The Venetian and take a gondola ride, then go for a walk on the Strip."

He paid the bill and found out the indoor portion of the ride closed at midnight, which gave them two hours. Rather than walk, Justin drove in case there was a long wait. It turned out to be a wise decision because the earliest available time was an hour later. The line had thinned out considerably by their scheduled time, and they were fortunate enough to have a private ride. Justin draped his arm around her, and she rested her head on his shoulder.

Siobhan didn't know if it was the romantic atmosphere of the ride, the feel of Justin's arm around her or the entire day, but all she wanted was to go back to the room. "Justin."

"Yeah, baby."

"Can we go back to the room after the ride?"

"Sure. Are you tired?"

She lifted her head, and their eyes met. "No."

She wasn't tired at all. In fact, she felt more energized than she had in a long while.

Chapter 10

Justin slanted his mouth over Siobhan's in an urgent kiss as soon as the hotel door closed. He removed her jacket and dropped it on the floor, and without breaking the seal of their mouths, he walked her backward until the backs of her legs hit the bed. He lowered her onto it and stretched his toned body on top of hers. Siobhan moaned, loving the feel of his weight.

"You don't know how many nights I fantasized about being here with you like this," Justin whispered against her lips as his hand snaked between their bodies to cup her full breast. He feathered kisses along her jaw, the column of her neck and the exposed portion of her chest.

A flurry of sensations rushed through Siobhan. "Justin." She had envisioned this moment, as well.

"I want to explore every part of your body." He came to his knees, brought her to a sitting position and pulled her shirt over her head. "Mmm, nice," he said of her apple-green lace bra, before dipping his head to gently bite her nipple through the fabric.

Electricity shot through her, and she moaned loudly. "I want you, too." She unbuttoned his shirt and ran her hand over the muscled wall of his chest. Siobhan darted her tongue out and swiped it across his nipple. His sharp intake of breath pierced the silence, and she repeated the action with its twin, eliciting a low moan from his throat.

"We have on way too many clothes," Justin murmured. He paused to pull the comforter back. "Lie back, baby." He lifted first one foot, then the other, and slipped her shoes off. Then he unfastened her slacks and slid them down and off to reveal matching panties. He caressed each leg, starting at her foot and working his way to her hips, then followed with his mouth.

Justin lifted his head briefly. "I gotta tell you, you are sexy as hell, and what you're wearing… I could look at you all night long. But I want to see it all." He hooked his thumbs in the waistband of her panties and slowly removed them. He reached behind her and, with one flick of his wrist, undid her bra. Siobhan's breasts sprang free, and he latched on to a hardened bud.

Every place on her body tingled. Justin mastered her body like someone who had been schooled in the art of pleasure. "What about your clothes?" Siobhan said breathlessly. She reached up and pushed his shirt off his shoulders. He rose and kicked off his shoes, then tossed the shirt aside and went to work on his pants, removing them and his briefs in one fluid motion. She thought his upper body impressive, but his strong thighs and tight buttocks, not to mention his engorged manhood, had her close to drooling.

He dug in his bag and retrieved condoms, tore one off and tossed the others on the nightstand. Justin rolled it over his length and came back to the bed. "Now, where was

I? Ahh, I think I was here," he said, swirling his tongue around her breasts and kneading them.

Siobhan wanted him inside her now. "Justin, I can't wait." She rotated her hips and closed her hand around his erection, but he shifted out of her reach.

"Relax, sweetheart, and just feel. We have all night."

He continued to torture and tease her breasts with his mouth while one hand feathered over her belly and lower still until he reached her center. He pushed her legs apart, parted her folds and slipped first one finger, then another one, inside her. She grew wetter and wetter with each bold stroke and arched into his hand. His fingers moved faster and faster, and when he added a third finger, Siobhan gripped the sheets and moaned loudly as a blinding orgasm tore through her.

Justin withdrew his fingers and kissed his way back up to her mouth. The kiss was seductive with a slow, drugging intimacy that had warning bells screaming in her head. She sensed something different in the way he kissed her, something that said this was more than just sex. She tensed.

"What is it, Siobhan?"

She shook her head quickly. "Nothing." How could she tell him that the emotions he roused in her frightened her? She could do sex, but with her track record, she didn't want to make the same mistake as before.

His expression turned serious. "If you've changed your mind, it's—"

"No." She swept her tongue into his mouth and captured his, conveying just what she wanted.

He groaned, positioned his body over hers, pushed at her entrance and buried himself to the hilt. Justin eased out to the tip and thrust again, establishing an easy rhythm. "So good," he murmured.

Each rhythmic thrust drew Siobhan further into his web of passion until she lost all sense of time and space. He kept up the pace for several minutes, and she whimpered when he withdrew.

He chuckled softly. "Don't worry. I got you, baby." He turned Siobhan on her side, came up to a high kneel, placed one thigh between hers and slid back in. "Tell me if you like this."

She cried out at the sweet invasion. In this position, he could go deeper and hit her G-spot with every stroke. He quickened his movements. Her cries grew louder, and her breathing came in short gasps. A spiraling sensation began low in her belly and swept her up like a tornado. Siobhan cried out as another orgasm ripped through her.

Justin threw his head back and let out a guttural groan as he found his own climax. "Siobhan." His body shuddered, and he called her name on a ragged moan. His head hung limp for a moment, and then he pulled out and collapsed on the bed beside her, his front to her back, draping an arm over her middle and snuggling close. "As soon as I catch my breath, I'll run some bathwater and we can soak in that huge tub."

"Mmm." That was the only word she could manage. Her heart thudded in her chest, and tremors still raced through her. The man not only could kiss, but also knew his way around a woman's body. She must have dozed off because she never heard Justin leave the bed or run the water. She wasn't the smallest person, but Justin lifted her in his strong arms as if she weighed nothing.

"How's the water?" he asked, lowering her into the tub.

"Fine."

He sat beside her, gathered her in his arms and pressed his lips against hers. "I like holding you in my arms."

"And I like you holding me in your arms." They relaxed for several minutes. Then he reached for one of the washcloths lying on the edge of the tub, wet it and let the water drizzle over her shoulders and back.

"I hope you don't mind me using the hotel's shower gel."

"No," she murmured, enjoying his ministrations.

Afterward, Justin led her back to the bed, hit the lights and snuggled behind her, his hand lightly caressing her hip and thigh. No other man had taken such an inordinate amount of time to please her, not even the man she was supposed to marry. She smiled. Maybe being with him wasn't all bad.

The shard of light peeking through the heavy curtains awakened Justin. He glanced over his shoulder at the clock, then back at the woman curled into his side. They had another three hours before checkout. He left the bed silently and went to the bathroom. He returned and crawled back into bed, being careful not to disturb Siobhan. It had been a long time since he'd had a morning after—he made a practice to avoid them—but for the first time, he didn't feel the restlessness that usually had him bolting for the door. In fact, he was stunned by how right it felt waking up next to Siobhan. His groin stirred with the memory of the previous night, and a smile spread across his lips.

Then he frowned. The sex had been great, and despite what she said about wanting him, he knew Siobhan still hadn't allowed herself to enjoy it fully. Justin didn't know whether it was because she'd been hurt badly in a previous relationship, or if it was just like she said—she never let go of her control. But now that he'd got a glimpse of her fire, he wished for nothing more than to unlock the passion she kept so tightly bound.

Siobhan shifted. Her eyes fluttered then opened, and she smiled.

Justin's heart did a little flip. "Good morning, beautiful."

"Good morning."

He kissed her lightly.

"Excuse me. I need to go to the bathroom."

He watched her naked curvaceous body as she passed, and he hardened immediately. He'd planned for them to have breakfast and then get on the road, but breakfast and the road would have to wait.

"What time are we heading back?" Siobhan asked as she climbed into bed again.

"After I get another taste of your sexy body," he answered, kissing her until she lay flat. His hand traveled over her smoother-than-silk skin, from her face to her neck, and finally settled on her breasts. Justin massaged the full mounds, then left her mouth, captured a pebbled nipple between his teeth and tugged gently, drawing a sharp cry from her. "You like that, baby?"

"Ooooh, yes." Her head dropped back, and her eyelids closed.

"That's good because today I'm going to make you scream." He slid down her body, hooked her left leg over his shoulder and placed a kiss on her knee. He trailed his tongue along her inner thigh to her warm, moist center, then mirrored his actions on her right leg. Justin repeated the action until she trembled and writhed beneath him, then plunged his tongue into her slick, wet heat.

"Justin," she chanted as his tongue moved faster and deeper.

He felt the moment she started to lock down her emotions and tried to scoot away, but he wasn't having it, not today. "Let it go, sweetheart."

"Noooo, I…I can't."

"Yes, you can. It's okay. Let go in my arms, Siobhan." He slid in two fingers and sucked the tiny bud between her legs, and she screamed his name, the sound like music to his ears. He lowered her legs, reached for and donned the condom he'd placed on the nightstand, and guided his engorged shaft into her body. He groaned as he sank deep within her tight walls. Justin reversed their positions, pulling her on top of him.

Siobhan leaned down to kiss him.

He cradled the back of her head and deepened the kiss, his tongue slipping into her mouth. "Ride me, baby," he whispered against her lips.

"I've never had the pleasure of riding."

"No? Well, there's a first time for everything. I want you to take control."

A spark lit in her eyes. She braced her hands on his chest, lifted her body.

Justin grabbed her hips and guided her down. She moved slowly at first, almost tentatively. Then something seemed to burst free in her, and she took him on a ride like he'd never experienced. Siobhan swiveled her hips and slammed down on him, her hands firmly gripping his shoulders. And each time she came down, he thrust up to meet and match her strokes, going deeper each time.

"I like this," she panted, arching her back and increasing the tempo, rocking the bed.

So did he. His eyes rolled to the back of his head, and she had him damn near ready to speak in tongues. But the sheer impact of how she was making him feel prevented him from uttering one coherent word. Her inner muscles clenched him, and he knew she was about to climax. He wanted them to come together. Holding her hips tightly, Justin pounded into her. The moment a gigantic explosion hit him, Siobhan let out a hair-raising scream. He quickly covered her mouth with his, absorbing the sound in a hard kiss. Their bodies bucked and shuddered for what seemed like hours before she collapsed on him.

Justin could feel the rapid pace of Siobhan's heart beating in rhythm with his. He wrapped his arms around her and marveled at how well she appeared to suit him. On some level, he'd known she had fire beneath her conservative exterior, but never did he expect her to turn out to be the completely uninhibited woman with whom he had just shared the best orgasm of his life.

When he could finally get his mouth to work, Justin said, "Damn, girl. You can take control anytime you want."

Siobhan lifted her head. "Good, because I like it up here so much you may never get me off." She raised an eyebrow and chuckled. "And I'm guessing by your response, you'd like another ride."

His arousal was instantaneous, and he laughed. "There are some things a man can't hide." His laughter turned into a groan of satisfaction when she rose above him and slowly, meticulously impaled herself on his rapidly growing erection.

"Let's see if I can make *you* scream this time," she said with a sultry wink.

Justin cursed and wondered if a man could die from too much pleasure.

An hour and a half later, showered and ready to check out, he stared at Siobhan in awe as she went in and out of the bathroom gathering her things. Sex with her went beyond his wildest dreams, and he got hard all over again thinking about those two last rounds.

"I think I have everything," she said, surveying the room.

He picked up both bags and headed for the door. Taking one last look around, he opened the door and let her precede him out. Rather than waste time standing in line, he had used the express checkout. After placing their small bags into the car, he and Siobhan had a quick breakfast in one of the hotel's restaurants then hit the road.

"What are your plans for the rest of the day?" he asked later.

"We're getting together for family dinner."

"Are you going early to help cook?"

"I'm supposed to be."

"We should make it back around three if we don't hit any traffic."

"But since we're talking LA, it's highly unlikely," Siobhan added with a shake of her head.

Justin laughed. They fell silent for a while, and then he said, "Can I ask why you're always so…so…?" He tried to find the right word without offending her.

"Uptight, controlling, bitchy."

He slanted her a quick glance. "You don't pull any punches with your words, do you?"

"Nope."

"Well, those words weren't exactly what I was going for. I was thinking more along the lines of reserved or guarded."

She shrugged. "It's just the way I am."

"That's not who you were for the past twenty-four hours— the complete opposite—and somehow, I don't think that woman just appeared out of thin air."

Out of the corner of his eye, he noticed her clenching her fists and suspected he might be pushing her too far. Justin reached for her hand. "For the record, both facets of your personality turn me on."

She didn't respond and he dropped the subject, not wanting to spoil the mood. Sooner or later, he'd find out who or what made her this way.

Chapter 11

Siobhan was still laughing when Justin drove up to her house and shut off the engine. "Justin, I can't thank you enough for these last two days. It's been a long time since I've had such a great time."

"See, I told you being kidnapped wasn't all bad."

"Yeah. I don't think many people have had such a pleasurable abduction."

"Then we'll have to do it again. Maybe you can kidnap me next time." Justin leaned close to her ear. "I'll even let you tie me up."

Her pulse leaped, and a rush of images from last night and this morning flashed across her mind. "You never know." She checked her watch and sighed. "I'd better go. I'm supposed to be at my parents' by now."

He got out of the car, retrieved her bag from the trunk and came around to her side. Taking her hand, he walked her to the door and waited while she unlocked it. "Thank you for spending the weekend with me." He set her bag down just inside the door.

She tilted her head for a kiss, and he didn't disappoint. He placed feather-like kisses along her jaw and the corners of her mouth. Her lips parted, and his tongue found hers, making sweeping, swirling motions in her mouth and driving her crazy in the process. His arm came up around her and he pulled her closer, their bodies pressed tightly together. Justin continued his intense exploration, unhurriedly. Siobhan broke off the kiss and sucked in a deep breath. "I have to go."

"I know," Justin said with a hint of reluctance. "I'll call you later."

She nodded and watched him lope back down the walkway to his car. She threw up a wave and closed the door. Smiling, she picked up her bag and hummed Michael Jackson's "You Rock My World" on the way to her bedroom.

Siobhan noticed the blinking red light on her answering machine and pressed the button.

"Siobhan, call me as soon as you get this."

She frowned upon hearing Brandon's solemn tone. The next message played.

"Where the hell are you, sis? I tried to call your cell and it went straight to voice mail."

She dug out her cell and powered it up, going directly into panic mode and thinking something had happened to one of her parents or siblings. There were two missed calls from Brandon, the first one similar to the ones left on her home phone. She listened to the second message.

"Shit, Vonnie. Everybody's worried about you. We got a call from Legal. Somebody is filing a lawsuit alleging one of our products failed and injured his wife. Call me as soon as you get this."

"Oh, no." Her stomach dropped, and guilt immediately surfaced. She should have stayed in town. And she shouldn't have let Justin talk her into turning off her phone. Her dad was going to be so disappointed and upset. Snatching up her purse, she rushed out to her car and sped over to her parents' house. She recognized all of her siblings' cars, along with Malcolm's motorcycle. She wished he wouldn't ride that thing. She let herself inside and followed the voices to the family room.

"Oh, Siobhan. Thank God." Her mother came to her feet quickly and engulfed Siobhan in a crushing hug. "Baby, are you okay?"

"I'm fine."

Brandon was across the room in a flash. "Do you know how many times I called you?" he yelled, towering over her. "Somebody's trying to ruin the company, and you're off doing who knows what. You should've been here."

"I had my cell turned off."

"Since when do you turn off your phone?"

Siobhan planted her hands on her hips. "Since yesterday," she shot back.

He took a step toward her.

Her father rose to his feet. "Brandon, sit *down*! Your sister doesn't need you jumping all over her."

"Who knows what this man is planning? We need to get on top of this now."

"Brandon," her father warned. "Siobhan, honey, is everything okay?"

"Yes, Daddy. I was out with a friend and lost track of time." He didn't need to know any more details of her weekend.

"A friend? Perhaps a nice gentleman?" her mother asked hopefully.

"Yes, Mom."

"Well, why didn't you invite him to dinner?"

"It's not like that. Anyway, what happened?" Siobhan caught Morgan's smile.

Morgan mouthed, "I want all the details."

"We don't know much right now," her father said, taking his seat again. He shot a look at Brandon. "We'll meet first thing tomorrow morning with Legal to get the details, then set something up with the media."

"I can set up a press conference as soon as we're done," Siobhan said.

"I called Gordon and asked him to start pulling information from newspapers and online. I want to know what's been said."

She scrubbed a hand across her forehead and dropped down on the sofa next to Malcolm. Not Gordon. "Daddy, I could have done all that."

"This couldn't wait," Brandon said.

Khalil threw up his hands. "Will you give it a rest, Brandon? You act like there was something she could have done. Didn't you just hear Dad say we're meeting *tomorrow*?"

Knowing all this still didn't ease Siobhan's guilt.

"I know, Siobhan," her father continued. "But you can't do it all, sweetheart."

Malcolm patted her knee. "Dad's right, sis. You're the boss. Delegate."

The conversation flowed around her, but she tuned it all out. The only words she heard were the ones in her head that told her she'd let her family down again.

Her mother held up a hand. "Nolan, there's nothing left to do about it today except pray. The rest will have to wait until tomorrow. Siobhan, you and Morgan come on in the kitchen and help me finish dinner."

Siobhan and Morgan followed their mother into the kitchen.

"Baby, don't you let Brandon get to you. You're entitled to your life." She opened the refrigerator.

"Thanks, Mom."

She glanced over her shoulder. "I do hope we get to meet this young man sometime soon."

Siobhan rolled her eyes. As much as she'd enjoyed this weekend, she had to cool it with Justin. She had more pressing matters.

Morgan giggled. "I hope so, too."

Siobhan ignored them and busied herself with seasoning the chicken.

She didn't talk much throughout dinner and excused herself to leave early. Justin called later that night, but she let it go to voice mail and tried to tamp down her desire to be with him. Not that it would work. At this point, nothing would satisfy the yearning that intensified by the minute... except more of him.

Justin hadn't felt this energized in a long while. The weekend with Siobhan had gone better than he'd planned, and he was still smiling about her excitement during the show. He enjoyed her open and playful side, and every time he remembered how she rode him, he was tempted to drive back to her house and try to coax her into one more round.

He left his bag on his bed and headed straight for his office. Justin worked on his slides for the next two hours, ensuring he had included all the pertinent details of his system and statistics of how the current models fared in the market. Once he was satisfied with the presentation, he took a break to call Siobhan. It went to her voice mail, so he pushed down the uncharacteristic longing and set up the demonstration he'd planned and tested it. Instead of the typical movement demo, he'd decided to show one of the temperature features—the one that currently worked. Although the system could tell the temperature inside the house and adjust it remotely if necessary, he continued to have some difficulties getting it to distinguish between people, pets or appliances. But by the time it came to market, he would have it figured out.

Justin tossed and turned all night. Between his excitement about the presentation and images of Siobhan's naked body atop his, he doubted he'd got more than three hours of sleep. He went for his usual run, which helped to clear his mind, made a stop at the bank and picked up some necessities from the grocery store. After putting the groceries away, he sent Siobhan a text and started gathering his equipment.

He pressed the button on his answering machine to listen to the messages he had put off from yesterday—two telemarketing calls that he promptly deleted. He went still in the middle of wrapping a cord when he heard the third message.

"Good morning, Mr. Cartwright. This is Gloria Avery calling from Gray Home Safety. There's been an emergency, and Mr. Gray will be unable to see you today. Please call me at your earliest convenience to reschedule. He sends his deepest apologies." She left a number, and he jotted it down.

"Damn," he muttered. He dropped the cord on the desk and picked up the phone. Ten minutes later, Justin hung up and released a deep sigh. The first available appointment wasn't until the following week on Thursday. Although frustrated, he hoped nothing serious had happened. It would, however, give him more time to work on the heat sensor problem.

And work on Siobhan.

Monday morning Siobhan was up and in her office by six. Her father had called Gordon and he'd be flaunting it in her face soon enough, but she planned to be ready for him. His resistance to use social media would work in her favor. Two hours later, she'd printed out stats and conversations from the various sites, placed them in a folder and made her way to the conference room. Just as she'd predicted, Gordon entered and came directly to where she sat. She'd give anything to be able to slap that smirk off his face.

"I see you dropped the ball again, Siobhan."

"How do you figure that?"

"If you were doing your job and not *unavailable* this weekend, your father wouldn't have had to call me to pick up the slack."

"He called you to start with the tasks usually assigned to the media *technician*, not the media *specialist*." Siobhan had to choke back a laugh at the man's stunned expression.

"Just because you're the boss's daughter doesn't give you the right to talk to me that way," he snapped. "I'm still your elder, and you will show me some respect."

She narrowed her eyes and lowered her voice to a harsh whisper. "Respect is a two-way street, *Gordon*. When you figure out how to do that, let me know. Until then, stay out of my way."

Before Gordon could reply, another member of her team passed by. Richard Harper had worked as the company's graphic designer since Siobhan was a teen and could pass for a middle-aged Ken doll.

"Morning, boss. Gordon." He winked at Siobhan.

"Good morning, Mr. Harper." She'd purposely used Richard's last name as a gesture of respect.

Gordon looked as if he would explode at any moment. He gave them once last glare and stormed off.

Richard chuckled and took the seat next to her. "I see he's still at it."

"Always." They shared a smile.

Minutes later, Mr. Whitcomb called the meeting to order. "Nolan will be here in a moment, but let's get started. Legal, what are we looking at?"

Siobhan listened and found out that a man whose wife

fell and was injured in the shower when one of the company's handrails broke had filed the suit. He detailed the woman's injuries and mentioned that the man planned to call one of the local TV stations to air his grievance.

Her gaze strayed to the doorway when her brothers and father walked in. Although Malcolm and Khalil didn't work directly for the company, they had seats on the board and attended most of the meetings.

She waited until he paused then asked, "Do we know how long the rails had been installed?"

"Best information we could gather so far indicates a day or two."

"Were the original packaging and materials recovered?" Brandon asked.

"Yes. We've also asked for a receipt and medical records."

"Gordon, what did you find out?" her father asked.

Gordon shot Siobhan a smug look then walked to the front of the conference room.

She shook her head. Every other person had spoken from their seats, but not him. He clearly thought more highly of himself than he should have. He finished providing the information he'd gathered from mainstream media and sat.

"Nicely done, Gordon," her father said.

"I took the liberty of searching social media to see what types of conversations were being had," Siobhan started, "and found that one particular article had been shared forty-seven times on Facebook, with an average of ninety-one comments. Roughly seventy-five percent of those comments expressed confidence in our products. On Twitter, I found thirteen different articles, but less than fifty comments, mostly positive. I issued a general statement on both sites."

"Brilliant move, Siobhan," Mr. Whitcomb said. "We've got to keep up with the times and go where the people are."

"Thank you, sir. I feel it's important that we utilize all

platforms to communicate with the public." She curbed the urge to make eye contact with Gordon.

"Siobhan, when can we have a press release ready?" her father asked.

"In an hour. I'll stop by your office first."

He nodded. "Morgan, I want you to take the lead on this case."

The shocked look on Morgan's face was priceless. Morgan had recently confided to Siobhan that she didn't want to be an attorney for the company, but rather a sports agent.

Her father stood. "Thank you for your hard work. The meeting is adjourned."

On the way to her office, Siobhan's cell phone buzzed. Her steps slowed upon seeing a text from Justin.

Hey, Siobhan. Hope your week is off to a great start. I enjoyed this weekend and can't wait to do it again soon.

Just reading his words sent heat spiraling through her. Pocketing the phone, she continued to her office. She couldn't deal with him right now.

By seven o'clock that evening, Siobhan was still sitting at her desk. She rested her head against her chair and closed her eyes. The press conference had gone off without a hitch, and all the releases had been distributed as scheduled, but she was exhausted. Her cell rang, and she didn't have to look at it to know it was Justin calling. She *had* dropped the ball last weekend and didn't want to think of what could have happened if it had been something more immediate, or worse, if one of her family members had got hurt again.

"I see you're still here."

She spun around in her chair and glowered at Brandon in her doorway. "What do you want, Brandon?"

"It's after seven."

"And? First you tell me I'm staying too late, and then you all but tell me I'm not doing my job. Which one is it?" she asked with annoyance.

His lips settled into a grim line. "That's not what I said, Siobhan."

She jumped from her chair, rounded the desk and pointed a finger at him. "*Yes*, you did. You made it sound like I let Dad down."

Brandon let out an exasperated sigh. "What are you talking about?" They were both yelling now.

"Oh, come on, Brandon. Cut the crap. You know what you said. *Somebody's trying to ruin the company, and you're off doing who knows what*," she mimicked.

"Vonnie, that's not what I meant."

"Then why did you say it?" Angry tears stung her eyes.

He ran a hand over his head. "I was upset, worried… I don't know. But I never said you let Dad down, and I don't know why you would think something like that," he added softly.

She swiped at a tear that escaped.

"I'm sorry." He groaned. "Please don't cry."

"I'm not crying. I'm mad."

"I know. You can hit me." He tapped his chest. "Go ahead."

Siobhan seriously considered taking him up on the offer. Growing up, when one of the boys did something to upset their sisters, they let the girls hit them once in the chest to even the score. But they weren't kids anymore. "Go home," she mumbled and went back to her chair.

"Not until you leave. I know I'm the last person you want to see, but I'm not leaving you here alone."

Not having the strength to argue, Siobhan packed up and went home. After having leftover chicken from Sunday's dinner, she trudged down the hall to her room and flopped down on the bed. Out of the corner of her eye, she spied the weekend bag she had never unpacked, which reminded her that she needed to wash at least one load of clothes. Standing again, she placed the bag on her bed and emptied the dirty garments.

At the bottom lay the bag holding her two T-shirts from the Michael Jackson show, and with it all the memories of that magical weekend. Emotions that she worked hard to keep at bay struggled to rise to the surface, and she pushed them down. Reaching for her cell, she sent Justin a short message. She couldn't handle these feelings right now and didn't know if she would ever be ready for them.

The remainder of Justin's day went downhill. He spent the next several hours rewriting some codes and adjusting the sensors, but made two mistakes and had to start over. Siobhan had finally sent him a text that read: We should slow things down. No explanation, no nothing, and she wouldn't answer his phone call, which added to his frustration. He racked his brain trying to come up with a reason. Had he said or done something? She said she had enjoyed the weekend, so when had things changed?

It was close to eleven o'clock when he finally went to bed. He fell across the bed fully clothed and dropped into a restless sleep. Two hours later, he woke up hard and reaching for Siobhan. Rolling onto his back, Justin let out a loud groan. Why couldn't he stop thinking about her long enough to sleep? *Probably because I don't know what I've done wrong.* For the second night in a row, she invaded his peace of mind. He couldn't have another night like this one, not if he expected to get any work done.

Tomorrow he was going over to her house, even if it meant waiting all night.

Chapter 12

"Have you found out any other information about the lawsuit?" Siobhan asked Morgan as they ate a late lunch on Tuesday.

"Nothing more than what was disclosed in the meeting. We're still waiting on the reports."

"How do you feel about Dad asking you to take the lead?"

Morgan tossed her fork down and blew out a long breath. "I really don't want to do it. You know I don't have any intentions of making this my career."

"I know, but it'll give you some good experience for when you get your first sports client."

"I hope it happens sometime in this century. Unless it's a woman's sport, most athletes won't even look my way, like I don't know as much or *more* than they do about football."

Siobhan chuckled. "Hang in there. You'll get your chance. Do you have your dance class tonight?" Morgan taught tap, jazz and hip-hop at her friend's studio.

"No class tonight, but Brooke and I are meeting to start

the choreography for the summer show. It's going to be so good. We're thinking about highlighting the talents of one musical giant, but haven't decided who yet."

"What about Michael Jackson?" Siobhan asked nonchalantly.

Morgan sat straight up. "Ooh, he's *perfect*. And why are you smiling like that?"

"Huh?"

"You heard me. And you never said who you were with over the weekend."

"Justin showed up at my house Saturday morning and said he was there to kidnap me."

"Sounds like my kind of man. Where did you go?"

"We had breakfast, went over to the Santa Monica Pier for a while and ended up in Vegas."

Morgan's mouth dropped. *"Vegas?"*

"Yes." She told her sister how she had mentioned wanting to go back in one of her and Justin's conversations, and in another one talking about her love of Michael Jackson.

"So, based off what you'd told him in some random conversations, he remembered, drove you to Vegas—"

"*And* took me to see the Michael Jackson Cirque du Soleil show. It was phenomenal."

"That smile says the show wasn't the only phenomenal thing. Is he good in bed?"

"Morgan!" Siobhan's head whipped around to see if someone at a nearby table had overheard.

"Well, is he?"

She nodded.

"Girl, you'd better hold on to a man like that."

Siobhan's smile faded.

"Come on, Vonnie. I know you're not still tripping over Arthur. And we all know you still blame yourself for his lies."

"That's not true. And I'm over Arthur. Besides, it's not like that with Justin and me."

"If it isn't true, then there should be no reason why you and Justin can't have a great relationship. No man is going to go all out like that for some fly-by-night hookup."

"How do you know? Men do all sorts of things to get what they want. That's why I gave him Mom's maiden name as my last name."

Morgan shook her head. "You what? That's just wrong."

"Anyway, we're supposed to be talking about your show."

Morgan just smiled and continued to eat.

Back in her office, Siobhan had difficulty concentrating on writing a press release. Morgan's words rang in Siobhan's ears, and thoughts of the past came rushing back. That mess with Arthur was her fault. She shouldn't have been so gullible and put his name on her accounts. Granted, he had added her name to his, as well, but she found out he had opened the account one day before he took her over and not four years prior, as he'd said.

And Malcolm… If Siobhan had stayed home, Malcolm might not have fallen off his bike because she always watched her younger siblings when they played outside. Her parents didn't say anything when they arrived, but Siobhan knew what they were thinking. She was the oldest, the one they'd left in charge, and it was her responsibility to protect her siblings.

She had spent the past sixteen years ensuring her parents never had a reason to fault her for anything else. Her work ethic was impeccable, and aside from her farce of a relationship, she'd done well. Now there was Justin. Everything about the way he behaved with her revealed that what he wanted went far beyond the occasional liaison they'd agreed upon at the beginning. And for a moment, she let herself fantasize about what being with him long-term might be like.

Shaking herself mentally, she refocused her attention on the blank computer screen. What typically took her less than half an hour to complete stretched to three times longer. Siobhan had planned to stay late today, but with her mind wandering, she realized it would be a waste of time and energy. She shut down her computer and placed the flash drive in her tote, in case she felt like doing some work tonight. Minutes later, she sat behind the wheel of her car listening to one of the smooth R & B stations on satellite radio.

Her heart went into overdrive when she spotted a figure sitting on her porch as she approached her house. "What the…?" She trailed off when she got closer and recognized it was Justin. What was he doing here? Siobhan assumed, since he hadn't responded to her text, that he agreed that they should back off. She parked in the driveway and got out.

Justin stood, met her halfway and eased the tote from her arm. "Hey."

"Hey." He followed her up the two steps and into the house. "What are you doing here?"

"I came to apologize."

She stopped walking and turned back, her brows knit in confusion. "For?"

He shrugged. "For whatever. I don't know what happened between Sunday and when you sent me that text, but I'm sorry."

Siobhan wanted to stomp her foot. Why was he always so…so…*nice*? She pointed to a chair. "You can set that bag down."

"Did I do or say anything, Siobhan?"

"There was an emergency at my job, and I didn't get the message—"

"Because I convinced you to turn your cell off." He ran an agitated hand over his head, paced briefly and then took her hands. "I am so sorry, Siobhan. I just wanted you to have a few minutes of downtime because you work so hard. I never intended to cause you any trouble with your job."

He seemed so miserable that Siobhan felt bad for not calling him. "It's not your fault, Justin."

"Yes, it is. If I hadn't insisted…" He shook his head.

"It's fine, Justin, really. You didn't cause me any problems. Everything has been handled."

"Are you sure?"

"Positive." She smiled to put him at ease.

"So, what was that text about? I thought we were getting along fine. Are you having regrets about last weekend?" He stroked a finger down her cheek. "Because I don't have one regret."

"No, but…"

"But what?"

"I'm not sure where this is leading or what it means."

"Sweetheart, it's leading anywhere we want it to go."

"I thought you just wanted to have a good time with no attachments."

"I know I said that in the beginning, and at the time, I meant it. But I'm not so sure that's all I want anymore."

What if she couldn't give him more? She tried to ignore the anxiety weighing on her chest thinking about the negative possibilities. "I don't know, Justin."

His eyes softened in empathy. "He hurt you badly, didn't he? It's okay—you don't have to answer that."

How did he know? Going through that pain topped her list of why committed relationships were bad news, and it was why she always held back a part of herself. But her feelings for Justin had taken on a life of their own and scared her to death.

Justin tilted her chin and locked his gaze on hers. "Understand this—we can go as slow as you need, but I like you, Siobhan Hunter, and I believe there's something growing that neither of us anticipated."

Siobhan felt a twinge of guilt at the mention of her name. "Slow is good."

"Whatever you need." He kissed her. This one was soft and promising. He wrapped his strong arms around her, pulled her closer to the fit of his body and changed the intensity of the kiss. His tongue thrust in and out over and over again in an explosion of passion that staggered her.

She melted into him and felt the pulse of his erection pressed firmly against her. They were losing control. The kiss gentled and ended with nibbles on her bottom lip and neck.

"Sorry. We're supposed to be going slow," he husked out, transferring his kisses to the shell of her ear. At length, he lifted his head. "Do you want to get some dinner?"

"I took out a couple of chicken breasts to thaw this morning. You're welcome to stay."

"I'd like that."

"Let me change out of these clothes, and I'll be right back." He smiled, and that dark, penetrating gaze fixed on hers. Siobhan's heart rate quickened. She was falling, and fast.

Justin sat in one of the armchairs while waiting for Siobhan and cursed under his breath. His impulsivity could have cost Siobhan her job. Although she said everything worked out, it still bothered him just the same. She had every right to be angry with him, and he wouldn't have blamed her if she had tossed him out on his butt. Had he been out of the corporate workforce so long that he'd forgotten what it was like to be ruled by a time clock? He would be more careful in the future because meeting her brought a spark back to his life that he'd lost, and he didn't intend to lose it again.

"Okay. Let me see what I can come up with for this chicken."

He stood at the sound of Siobhan's voice behind him and trailed her to the kitchen. "What were you planning to do with it?"

She shrugged. "Grill, broil, sauté—I have no idea."

Justin laughed. "Sounds like me most days."

"What do you think?"

"Do you have some chili powder and cumin?"

Siobhan walked over and opened a cabinet. "Yep."

"What about bell peppers and onions?"

She moved to the refrigerator and checked. "I have two onions. Will red and yellow peppers do?"

"They will. If you have a grill pan, we can make fajitas."

"Yum. I haven't had fajitas in a while." She retrieved a cutting board and grill and sauté pans. "Since this was your bright idea, I'll let you season and cook the chicken, and I'll take care of the onion and peppers." She snapped her fingers and went back to the refrigerator. "Oh, wait. I know I have some," he heard her mumble. She held up a package. "Tortillas. Can't have fajitas without them."

They worked in companionable silence until Siobhan turned on the music. "Jazz, huh?"

"Sometimes after a long day, I need to hear something soothing, and contemporary jazz always relaxes me. Two of my favorites are Boney James and Brian Culbertson, as you can hear." She had selected a playlist featuring both artists.

Justin filed that information away in his brain for future use. Twenty minutes later, they sat down for dinner. She bowed her head and recited a short blessing, and he followed suit.

"Oh, my goodness. This is *so* good. You have to give me the spice rub recipe you used. The next time my siblings and I get together, I'm cooking this." She held up her fajita.

"I'll write it down for you before I leave."

"I might have to sample some of your other dishes."

Unknowingly, she had just given him the opening he'd been looking for. "Actually, I wanted to invite you over to my house on Saturday for dinner. If the weather holds, I can fire up the grill and we can eat outside on my deck. And you can bring your phone," he added quickly.

She chuckled. "Thanks. I'd like that."

They fell quiet for a while, and then Justin said, "Can I ask you a question?"

Siobhan hesitated briefly. "Okay."

"Why do you work so hard and such long hours? I mean, I know companies often demand a lot of time, but you seem to go far above the call of duty. Is someone hassling you and you're working because you think you need to prove something?"

She took a sip of the lemonade she'd made before answering. "Is that what you think?"

He nodded. "You remind me a lot of how I used to be. I put so much pressure on myself to do well because one, I didn't want to be a failure, and two, I wanted to make my parents proud."

"I forgot you're the oldest, so you know how it is." She ran her finger around the rim of her glass and spoke in a faraway voice. "My parents left us at home one afternoon when I was seventeen. They were meeting friends for lunch. Usually, I was the one they put in charge, but on this day, my two best friends asked me to go to the movies. I went. And I came home two hours later to flashing red lights and my baby brother unconscious and bleeding. He had fallen off his bike—always the daredevil," she said with a sad smile. She took a deep breath. "Anyway, he ended up with a concussion and had to get twelve stitches for a gash near his temple. If I had just stayed home... I let my parents and my brothers and sister down."

His heart broke for her, and he grasped her hand. "Baby, you can't possibly believe any of that was your fault. It was an *accident*." Justin left his chair and hunkered next to her. "All this time you've been trying to make up for something that you couldn't have prevented. That's a heavy burden for one person to carry. Take it from someone who knows. During a couple of my teen years, I stayed in trouble, but seeing what it did to my parents made me do a total one-eighty. Only this time, I worked myself into the ground trying to prove to them that I had changed.

"Three weeks of constant headaches sent me to the doctor. My blood pressure was so high, the doctor said she was surprised I hadn't had a stroke. At twenty-four years old, I was this close—" he put his thumb and index finger together "—to potentially dying. Sweetheart, you have got to let this go, or it will eat you alive."

"I'm trying, but it's hard."

"I know it is. It took some time for me to find some balance. But a decade later, I'm better, and hopefully wiser. If there's anything I can do to help—whether you want me to listen or just hold you—I'll do it."

"Thank you."

He rose, kissed her temple and returned to his chair. They finished their dinner without speaking, both lost in thought. Afterward, he sat and held her.

An idea came to him. He knew exactly what she needed to help her relax. He smiled. This was going to be good.

Chapter 13

Siobhan ran from the bathroom to catch her ringing phone, thinking it was Justin. "Ow!" She let out a loud groan when her foot connected with the edge of the nightstand. Biting back another moan, she lifted the receiver.

"Girl, I haven't talked to you since the party," Kendra said after Siobhan's greeting.

"I know. Hopefully nothing else happens, and we can meet for lunch this week." She sat on the side of the bed and rubbed her aching foot.

"What are you doing tonight?"

"Justin is picking me up in an hour, and we're having dinner at his house."

Kendra screamed. "You've been holding out on us! Hold on, hold on."

"Kendra? Kendra?" She shook her head.

"Hello?"

"Cynthia?" Siobhan said.

"Yeah. Siobhan, what's going on?"

"Siobhan's getting her groove back with Justin—that's what's going on," Kendra cut in. "Tell us everything, and don't leave anything out."

"Ooh, so you guys *are* dating," Cynthia said. "You should have seen them at your party, Kendra. Justin has it bad for Siobhan."

"Oh, brother." Siobhan repeated what she had told Morgan about their weekend, but had to stop every other sentence because Kendra kept asking questions.

"Ooh wee, kidnapped," Cynthia squealed. "That is so romantic."

Kendra whistled. "So how was the sex?"

"Who said we slept together?" Siobhan asked.

"Just answer the question. We know you did. It must have felt real good to dust the cobwebs off."

"Really, Kendra? Dust the cobwebs off?"

Cynthia laughed. "Well, it has been a while for you, girl, so…"

"It was good—better than good," she confessed.

"I knew it. I told you that night at the gala," Kendra boasted. "Cynthia, he's coming to pick her up for dinner *at his place*."

"He takes you on a whirlwind trip to Vegas and to see a show featuring one of your favorite musical artists, all from a conversation, *and* he cooks? Siobhan, Justin sounds like a keeper."

Admittedly, the man was setting the bar pretty high, but she wouldn't say he was a keeper, at least not yet. Siobhan couldn't wait to see what he whipped up for dinner tonight. She gasped. "I have to go. Justin is going to be here in ten minutes, and I'm not even dressed."

"Have fun," Cynthia and Kendra chorused.

"And we'll be waiting to hear the details next week at lunch," Kendra added.

"Yeah, yeah, I know." She hung up and dashed around

the room getting dressed. Her foot was still hurting, and she had to change shoes at the last minute. In the bathroom, she applied moisturizer to her natural curls and checked her makeup. The doorbell rang promptly at five, the time he'd told her he would arrive. She liked a man with good time management skills.

She opened the door. "Hey, come on in."

Justin entered and kissed her. "How was the rest of the week?"

Siobhan laughed. He was as bad as Brandon. "Busy, but I was out of the office by seven, at the latest."

"Glad to hear it."

"Let's go," she said with a shake of her head and walked out the door.

He placed his hand over his heart. "I'm just trying to do my part to keep you from working yourself to death."

She rolled her eyes. "Whatever, Justin." But she was smiling.

They chatted amicably during the drive, and Siobhan hid her surprise when he took her to one of the more up-scale neighborhoods. He had mentioned having a couple of safety products on the market, and by the looks of his home, they had to be performing well. He parked in the circular driveway and shut off the engine.

"Well, this is it."

"How long have you lived here?"

"Almost five years," he answered, getting out of the car and coming around to her side.

Siobhan was confused. From their conversation at her house last week, she estimated Justin's age to be somewhere around thirty-four, which meant that he had purchased the house before he turned thirty. Her curiosity peaked when he opened the door and her feet touched the glossy natural maple hardwood floor. He had an open layout, and each room flowed seamlessly into the next one. She walked over and ran her hand across the unique stone fireplace in the family room. "This is beautiful."

"Thanks. I'll give you a tour and then start dinner."

She followed him through the stunning home with four bedrooms, each with a private bath, and she saw two additional half baths—one off the kitchen and the other near the door leading to the backyard. The exquisitely crafted master retreat had a sitting area, fireplace and a luxurious spa-like bath. "Were you married before?"

Justin's brow lifted, and he folded his arms across his chest. "No."

"You've lived in this huge house by yourself this entire time?"

"Yes," he answered with a chuckle.

"It's kind of large for just one person."

"I could say the same about yours."

"No. I only have three bedrooms and nowhere near the square footage of this place. Besides, I have four siblings, and one or all of them might end up staying the night."

"Same here. In fact, that second bedroom with all the purple is Jocelyn's. She claimed it two months after I moved in and spends parts of the summer here."

"So, what's for dinner?"

He burst out laughing. "Woman, you can change a subject on a dime." He led Siobhan to the kitchen and directed her to a stool at the bar. "We're having steaks, corn with chili lime butter roasted in the husk, some sliced potatoes and a salad. Everything will be cooked on the grill except the salad."

"Ooh, that sounds delicious. What do you want me to do?"

"Sit your beautiful self right there and keep me company." He pointed to a stool. "Would you like a glass of wine?"

"Sure."

"I have a sauvignon blanc, Chardonnay or Merlot."

"Merlot, please."

Justin poured them each a glass and went about the dinner preparations. Once the food had been placed on the grill, they relaxed with their wine on the deck.

Over dinner, they talked more about their childhoods and respective jobs. He shared openly about developing video games in college with his friend and working his first job at a software company. Siobhan's conversation around her job stayed very general because she had withheld her true identity, a fact that had begun to bother her more and more.

Later, he stood and extended his hand. "Come sit with me." They moved from the table to a lounger, and Justin pulled her down onto his lap. He tightened his arms around her and kissed the side of her neck. "I've been waiting to hold you all night." He shifted her until she lay in the crook of his arm and slanted his mouth over hers. "I like the T-shirt, but I like what's under it even more," he whispered against her lips. She had worn the T-shirt he'd bought in Vegas.

His hand searched under her shirt and bra, baring her breasts to the cool evening air. Siobhan sucked in a sharp breath at the contrasting warmth of his tongue circling and teasing first one nipple then the other. His hand left her breasts and made a path down her front, where he unbuttoned and unzipped her jeans and slipped his hand inside her panties. She squirmed and writhed against the solid bulge beneath her bottom, wanting and needing to get closer to him. She pushed his shirt up and trailed her fingers over the smooth wall of muscles in his abs and chest.

Justin stilled her hips. "Not right now," he husked out.

Siobhan left his lap and planted her hands on her hips. "Then stop playing and make love to me."

"Whatever the lady wants." Taking her by the hand, he led her to his darkened bedroom. "Stand right here."

"Are you going to turn on the lights? And what are you

doing?" she asked. She could barely make him out in the shadows kneeling on the other side of the room.

"Patience, baby."

A moment later the ceiling was flooded with tiny white lights resembling the night sky filled with stars. In one corner sat a larger dim light that she guessed was supposed to be the moon. She gasped and brought her hand to her mouth. "I don't believe it," she said, turning in a slow circle. "How did you…? Why did you…?"

Justin came and stood in front of her, resting his hands on her waist. "Remember after the movie—black velvet night, millions of stars in the sky, the moonlight playing over your naked body and—" he pressed the button on a remote in his hand "—the sounds of the waves crashing against the shore. Since I couldn't coax you outdoors, I decided to bring the beach inside."

The sounds of the ocean filtered into the room through hidden speakers. "I don't know what to say. It's…it's *wonderful*. I can't believe you went through all this fuss just for…sex."

He framed her face and rested his forehead against hers. "It's not *just sex*, Siobhan. Not anymore. It's something else, something different. You feel it, don't you?"

Siobhan closed her eyes, clenched her teeth and tried to shove the truth of his words to the side. *No!* She didn't want to *feel*. Allowing feelings always ended with her heart being shattered.

"Tell me I'm not the only one, baby. I need to hear you say it."

"No, you're not," she finally confessed. She heard his sigh of relief at the same time he slanted his mouth over hers in a scorching kiss that left her aching with need.

Justin divested Siobhan of her clothes in a matter of seconds, pulled back the covers and lowered her to the bed.

The magical kisses started again, and she held his head in place, taking control and devouring his mouth.

He shuddered and broke off the kiss, his breathing ragged. "Be right back. I need one more thing." She moaned in frustration, and he chuckled.

He came back a few minutes later with a small bottle of honey. Siobhan sat up. "What are you going to do with that?"

A wicked grin covered his mouth. "I'm going to pour this all over your body and lick off. Every. Drop."

Her heart skipped a beat, and her clit pulsed.

Justin placed the bottle on the nightstand, removed his clothes and donned a condom. He climbed onto the bed and reached for the bottle.

She watched as he poured a small amount on his finger and smeared it on her lips. He leaned forward and swiped his tongue from one corner to the other. Siobhan captured his tongue and sucked hard, tasting the sweetness of the honey mixed with remnants of the wine and making him groan. He lifted the bottle and drizzled the warm liquid over her breasts, belly and at the juncture of her thighs. Slowly, meticulously, he charted a path with his tongue, pausing to torment the sensitive peaks of her nipples and continuing to her belly button.

"Mmm. You taste so good."

Siobhan had never experienced such intense sensations and couldn't stop the moans spilling from her lips. Each tantalizing lick and suckle had every nerve ending in her body tingling. His tongue made one long swipe across her clit. She cried out, and her hips flew off the bed.

"And so damn sweet," Justin murmured as he plunged his skilled tongue deep inside.

She trembled and gyrated her hips to his erotic rhythm. His tongue moved faster while his thumb circled the tiny nub. She felt her body tense, and seconds later she screamed as bolts of ecstasy shot through her. She shuddered uncontrollably. Justin moved up her body and entered her with one driving thrust. She arched up to meet him and wrapped her legs around his waist. He delved deeper with each measured stroke. Needing him to move faster, she squeezed her muscles around his shaft.

His breath hissed out of him. "Don't do that."

"Faster," she panted.

His eyes flashed, and he increased the pace. "Is this what you want?"

"Yesss." She clutched his back and tightened her legs around him.

"What about this?" Justin pulled out, flipped her over and up on all fours, then thrust back inside.

He plunged into her and she threw her hips back, matching his fluid movements. The tension built in her again and she came wildly, explosively.

Justin followed her over the edge with a loud shout. "Siobhan!" he called almost reverently. He placed a kiss in the center of her back and drew them down to the bed.

It took several minutes for their breathing to slow. The sounds of the ocean filtered into her consciousness. Siobhan chuckled tiredly. "I totally forgot about those ocean sounds."

She felt the low rumble of Justin's laughter against her back. "So did I, but then again, the only sounds I wanted to hear were your screams of passion."

She had certainly made lots of those. She was amazed by what he had done, and secretly pleased, but it complicated things. All her efforts to remain emotionally distant weren't working. She stared up at the twinkling lights and lost another piece of her heart.

Justin propped up on his elbow next to Siobhan, still in awe of their lovemaking. His gaze roamed over her naked body. Just as he'd anticipated, the subtle lighting shimmering on her satiny skin made for an alluring picture.

He watched the rise and fall of her chest as she slept. Her features were relaxed, and a slight smile played around the corners of her mouth. He lay back on the pillow and stared at the ceiling. He had tried to keep it about the physical, but the insistent tug on his heart wouldn't allow it. But was he ready for a serious commitment? He sighed heavily. He had to decide what he wanted, and soon, because the last thing he needed to do was hurt Siobhan. He closed his eyes and snuggled closer to her.

He dozed off and woke to the feeling of something dripping on his chest. Siobhan sat on her knees with a seductive smile, holding the bottle of honey. She dragged her finger through the sticky puddle and, holding his eyes, slowly sucked it into her mouth. Justin muttered a curse.

"Can I have a taste?"

Without waiting for his reply, she leaned down and licked his chest clean. He hardened immediately. She squirted some on his shaft and caught the portion running down the side with her tongue. His arousal level shot straight through the roof. His abdominal muscles contracted, and his breathing grew ragged. She swirled her tongue from base to tip over and over, then sucked him in deeply, driving him out of his mind. Justin swore hoarsely as her mouth moved up and down his length. Minutes later, a tingling started somewhere around his feet, and his orgasm sped through him with the force of a tsunami. He yelled out her name.

As he lay trying to catch his breath, he realized there was no way he would be able to let her go.

Chapter 14

Siobhan sat staring at her computer daydreaming about her night "under the stars." And that honey. She would never see honey the same way again. Her cell buzzed, and she knew without looking that it was Justin. She had begun to look forward to his daily messages. Picking it up, she pressed a button and read: Morning, sunshine! Hope your day is off to a good start. BTW, I think my new favorite meal is honey...and you. Heat thrummed between her legs. Feeling bold, she typed back: My day is fine. Hope ur having a great one, too. As far as a favorite meal, I may need to sample it again just to be sure. A naughty image filled her mind, and she smiled.

"Maybe I should come back some other time."

Siobhan's head popped up. "Oh. Hey, Brandon." She tossed the cell on her desk. "What's up?"

He angled his head thoughtfully. "You tell me." He entered and closed the door.

She waved him off. "Nothing. I'm just working on a new campaign for the rails to keep customer confidence up."

Brandon lowered his tall frame into a chair. "That's not what I'm talking about and you know it. Are you still seeing that guy?"

"Are you still seeing that woman?"

"I'm not sitting at my desk smiling at my cell phone. And I bet if I were to take a look, I'd find some sappy message from the guy."

"And you would know this how?"

"Siobhan, stop answering me with a question," he said with exasperation. "I hate when you do that. We're not in a press conference."

She had perfected the art of deflection, but as of late, it hadn't worked with any of her siblings. "Yes," she admitted.

"Is it serious?"

"I don't know. It wasn't supposed to be, but now…"

"Do you think he's after your money, like that other asshole?" He frowned.

"No. He doesn't know who I am." At Brandon's confused look, she explained, "I told him my name was Siobhan Hunter." She dropped her gaze. "I haven't got the nerve to tell him the truth. But judging from where he lives, I'd say he's financially stable."

"You do realize that if you plan to continue seeing him, you'll have to tell him sometime soon."

"I know, but…"

"But what? You're afraid he'll turn out to be like every other guy who wants a piece of Gray's?"

Siobhan nodded.

Brandon sighed. "I understand. I feel the same way. It's hard to know whether the person you're going out with is dating you for *you* or because of your name. Do you like him?"

"I do. I tell myself it's all about the physical, but it's starting to feel different, and I don't want to go through the same mess again."

He held up his hand. "Okay, first of all, you're my sister, and I don't want to think about you having sex with some dude."

Siobhan laughed. "Oh, come on, Brandon. I'm thirty-three. Did you think I'd never—"

"Stop! Just stop. I'm getting nauseous," he said with a pained look. "Anyway, like I was saying, you need to be careful. You may like him, but I know how men think. They'll say anything to get what they want."

She shook her head. Brandon lived by the mentality that no man would ever be good enough to date his sisters, and she was glad Khalil had a more balanced view. Malcolm, on the other hand, believed that as the oldest, Siobhan should be able to decide what she wanted. Of course, he had a totally different outlook when it came to his twin. He guarded Morgan like a hawk.

"And if you need me to talk to him, I will."

She gave him a sidelong glance. "Hold up, boy. You're getting carried away. Did you come by my office for a reason, like something work related?"

"Oh, yeah. Gordon was in my office spouting off at the mouth about you. He wants me to talk to Dad about how the company needs someone with more public-relations experience to be the face of the company, particularly now with the lawsuit."

Siobhan leaned back in her chair and folded her arms. "Gordon better keep his greasy, fat-bellied behind out of my business. He's about two seconds from me knocking him the hell out."

Brandon roared with laughter. "Greasy? Fat-bellied?" he choked out.

"It's not funny."

"Oh, yes, it is. Because you don't know the image that formed in my head."

"I'm serious. He's been in my face more times than I can count in the last few weeks."

Still chuckling, he shook his head. "You don't have to worry. I know you're the best person for this job, and so does Dad. Case in point—last week's meeting when he didn't bother to check social media. We have to stay on the cutting edge and can't afford to be stuck with twentieth-century technology." He stood and went to the door. "I just wanted to give you a heads-up. I'll see you later." He paused with his hand on the doorknob. "And remember what I said."

Siobhan ignored him and turned to her computer. Brandon must have forgotten, *again*, that she was the oldest, and she despised someone telling her what to do. She could handle Justin just fine.

Sitting in the conference room late Wednesday afternoon, Siobhan impatiently checked her watch again. She had planned to be gone by four thirty to get ready for her date with Justin, but unless a miracle happened and the meeting ended, she wouldn't make it out within the next thirty minutes. Turning her attention back to Mr. Whitcomb, she tried to focus on what the man was saying, but her mind kept wandering back to Justin and whether he was bringing more of that honey.

Forty-five minutes later he adjourned the meeting. *Hallelujah!* She was up and striding out of the building before anyone could stop her. She made it home and had just enough time to change before Justin arrived. She had expected them to fall into bed the moment they got back to her place from dinner, but he had other ideas. He'd rented a movie, one with no murders and stalkers, brought popcorn and suggested they enjoy a quiet evening.

It threw Siobhan off a little that he seemed to always

know what she needed. She had been on edge ever since talking with Brandon earlier in the week, and winding down in this way was perfect timing.

His hand idly caressed and massaged her neck, relaxing her further. She loved his hands on her and wondered how it would be having him here every night, doing just this.

Justin pulled Siobhan closer, feeling a contentment he had never experienced. They got along fine, had great conversations and similar tastes in music, but since sleeping together, he hadn't been able to think of anything else. He told her he felt something different, and although he wanted nothing more than to take her to bed, he needed to find out whether they had more than sexual chemistry piloting their relationship. Besides, he couldn't stay late tonight, and if they went anywhere near her bedroom, he wouldn't be leaving before morning.

His meeting with Gray Safety was tomorrow afternoon, and he was confident that the presentation and demo would go off flawlessly. The only thing he hadn't completed was the body-temperature element. He'd been focused on developing his relationship with Siobhan, but told himself he had plenty of time to get the problem solved.

"Now, this is more my speed," Siobhan said when the movie ended.

Justin laughed softly. "I figured you'd like this one better."

"Yeah, nobody jumping out at you, snatching you or shooting at you. I can handle a little bit of drama, but nothing like that first movie. I liked the girl's grandmother. She reminds me of mine—saying whatever comes to mind."

"Must be a trait of all grandmothers, but my mother is the same way."

"I think the older we get the less we care about what other people think, and just tell it like it is."

Justin smiled and shook his head. She already did that. What would she be like at that age?

"What are you smiling at?"

"You."

"What?"

"You're already very direct and 'tell it like it is,' so what are you going to do when you get older, chop people's heads off?"

Siobhan leaned away and socked him on the arm. "I beg your pardon. I do *not*. I'm very diplomatic."

He laughed out loud at that one. "I don't think so. Remember, you're the woman who told me the night we met, *How about we skip to the part where you hand me your business card and stop wasting my time?* And there wasn't nothing nice about the way you said it."

She laughed. "Hey, I was tired of all the crap I had been handed that night. You're lucky I let you finish that dance."

He sobered. "Yes, I was. And that you agreed to meet me the next morning for coffee," he added, touching his mouth to hers. "That you let me take you to dinner and a movie, and make love to you."

"Justin."

The atmosphere went from teasing to crackling with sexual tension in an instant. Justin's mouth descended on hers, hot and hungry. He lifted her to straddle his lap and continued to plunder her mouth and satisfy his need for the sweet lushness he always found within. His hands roamed down her back, to her full hips and around to cup her buttocks. He squeezed, kneaded and ground her against his throbbing erection.

The sound of his father's ringtone snatched him out of his sensual fog.

"You should get that," Siobhan said, still planting fleeting kisses on and around his mouth.

He sighed heavily and dug the phone out of his pocket. "Hey, Dad."

"Your mother is in the hospital," his father said without preamble.

Justin's heart jumped into his throat. "What happened?" he asked anxiously. Seeing his concerned expression, Siobhan slowly left his lap, sat next to him and grasped his hand.

"I don't know. I was out back, came inside and found her unconscious. They're running some tests right now."

"Is she conscious?"

"Yes, yes."

"I'll be there tonight," Justin said, coming swiftly to his feet. At this time of night, he could make the drive to Nevada without having to worry about traffic.

"Son, there's nothing you can do tonight. Why don't you wait until tomorrow?"

"Dad, that's not an option. Do Yvonne and Jocelyn know?"

"I talked to Yvonne a few minutes ago. She had called to say hello, so I filled her in. She's just as stubborn as you," his father groused. "Said her young man was driving her down."

"I'll call Joce and bring her with me. Call me if something changes before I get there."

His father released a deep sigh. "I will."

Justin disconnected and ran a weary hand down his face.

Siobhan stood next to him. "What's going on?"

"My mother passed out and is in the hospital. I have to go."

She nodded and gave him a strong hug. "Please be careful, honey, and give me a call when you get a chance. I'll be praying for her."

"Thanks, sweetheart. I will." He kissed her softly and then called his baby sister, who agreed to meet him at his house. He hung up and checked the time—ten thirty. With any luck, he could get home, pack and be on the road in an hour. He kissed Siobhan again and rushed out to his car.

Twice while driving home, he had to caution himself to slow down. He was going well over the speed limit, and being stopped by the police or getting into an accident wouldn't help his mom. Why had she passed out, and how long had she been lying unconscious?

"Dammit!"

Once again, he'd got distracted. He'd told himself he had time to work out the kinks in his system, but if he had worked longer and harder, or had taken an offer from one of the other companies that had shown interest, his father would have been alerted the moment she hit the floor.

Justin pulled into his driveway at the same time Jocelyn got out of her car.

She ran to him and threw her arms around him as soon as his foot hit the pavement. "Is Mom going to be okay?"

"She's going to be fine," he told her, wrapping her in a comforting hug. The fear in her eyes mirrored what he felt on the inside. But he kept his worry hidden for her sake. "Let me throw a few things in a bag, and we'll get going. Put your bag in the car."

"All right."

He left her to the task and went in through the garage. It took him less than fifteen minutes to pack and to grab his laptop and flash drives. He cursed. Seeing Mr. Gray's business card on the desk reminded him that he was supposed to meet with the man tomorrow. He stuck the card in his pocket, picked up the bag and left.

Justin stopped for gas and hit the highway fifty-two minutes after receiving his father's call.

"Did you have a business meeting tonight about one of your systems?" Jocelyn asked after a while.

"No. Why?"

"You're usually at home and in your office working during the week. You barely go out, unless it's for business or with Bobby."

That had been true before he met Siobhan. He'd spent less time working and more time playing in the past month than he had in the past year. And his mom was paying for it.

"Well?"

"Well, what?" His eyes left the road briefly to focus on her in time to see her cover her mouth in surprise.

"You were on a date, weren't you? I hope it's the same woman. I can't wait to tell Yvonne."

"I haven't said anything for you to tell."

"You don't have to. Your silence tells me *everything* I need to know. Big brother's got a girlfriend," she sang. "This must be getting serious since it's been over a month." She turned in her seat toward Justin. "Wait—she's not one of those crazy women who was calling you last year when you were up for that technology innovation award, is she?"

"No, Jocelyn. I've never mentioned it, and neither has she. I'm sure she knows nothing about it." Thinking back, he realized most of his and Siobhan's conversations steered clear of their respective jobs. Aside from a few general questions, he didn't know much about what she did or even where she worked. She had been very careful to say as little as possible.

"Hmm. She might have potential. What does she do?"

"She works in public relations."

"And she has a job. I'm impressed."

"Can we talk about something other than my personal life, please?"

Jocelyn laughed. "Sure—why not? How did your meeting go with the company interested in your alert system?"

"I haven't met with them yet. They had an emergency and postponed the meeting. We're supposed to meet tomorrow, but I'll call first thing in the morning to try to reschedule."

"Did you ever resolve the problem with the temperature?"

"No. If I had been more focused in the last month or two, I could have had it finished. And if I wasn't so stuck on partnering with Gray's, it might already be on the market. Then maybe Dad would have found Mom sooner." The tightness in his chest increased.

"Justin, don't start. You did the same thing after Grandpa died. And why would you even consider settling? Your alert system is so much better than anything I've seen—and you know I pay attention—so why would you cut corners and throw something out there? Think about how many lives will be saved because you took your time and, instead of putting out a good product, put out a great one. Mom and Dad would be really angry with you if they heard you talking like this."

"But—"

She laid her hand on his arm. "No buts. You used to tell me studying is good, but to always make time for something fun to clear my mind. That one piece of advice has helped me more than anything else these last three years. You have to live your life, too."

Justin heard her, he knew it, but it didn't ease his guilt. It was time to reassess his priorities. Maybe he wasn't as ready for a committed relationship as he believed.

Chapter 15

After less than three hours of sleep, Justin, Yvonne and Jocelyn were up and at the hospital by seven. He cracked open the door to his mother's room and saw his father asleep in a recliner. He turned and signaled his sisters to be quiet. He opened the door farther, and his heart lurched upon seeing his mother. Her normally healthy dark brown skin had paled, and she looked as if she'd lost several pounds since he had seen her two months ago.

He let his sisters take the two vacant chairs while he leaned against the wall.

"I don't like to see Mom like this," Yvonne whispered, tears filling her eyes.

Jocelyn nodded. "Me, either. I'm scared."

Seeing the tears in his sisters' eyes always did something to Justin. He couldn't take it when they cried. He hunkered down in front of them and took each of their hands. "I know you're scared. I am, too. But I know Mom is going to be fine. We have to stay strong for her and Dad, so no tears, you two. You know I can't handle it when you cry."

"This is exactly why I told your father not to call you," his mother said softly.

He shot to his feet, and his sisters rushed over to the bed.

"Mama, you scared us to death. Are you okay?" Yvonne asked.

"I'll be fine," she said with a tired smile. She reached for Jocelyn's hand. "Stop crying, baby. I'm all right."

Justin leaned down and pressed a kiss to her forehead. "Hey, Mom."

She cupped his face with her palm and frowned. "You look tired, Justin. Don't tell me you drove up here in the middle of the night."

He grinned sheepishly. "Okay, I won't tell you."

"Boy, I don't know what I'm going to do with you."

"What happened, Mom?"

"I've had this darn flu for the past couple of weeks. I thought it was getting better. Then two days ago, it came back again, fever and all. I was putting some dishes in the cabinet and got dizzy. Next thing I knew, your daddy was holding my head in his lap and I was on the floor. Turns out, I have an ear infection…and at my age."

"Did the doctor say how long you'd have to stay in the hospital?" Jocelyn asked.

"She said today or tomorrow. They want to make sure this fever goes down."

Justin placed the back of his hand on her forehead. "You still feel a little warm to me, so I'm guessing it'll be tomorrow."

She rolled her eyes. "I'd be much better in my own bed."

He shook his head. Same old Mom. "I'll be right back. I have to make a phone call." He found a waiting room and dialed Gray Home Safety.

"Good morning, Gray Home Safety. This is Gloria Avery. How may I help you?"

"Good morning, Ms. Avery. This is Justin Cartwright. I have an appointment with Mr. Gray this afternoon at three."

"Yes."

"I apologize for the short notice, but I had to leave town last night for a family emergency. My mother has been hospitalized. Is it possible for me to reschedule?"

"Certainly, Mr. Cartwright. Hold on just one moment while I check the schedule. I have an availability next Tuesday at eleven or Friday at ten."

"I'd like the Friday appointment, please." That would give him time to make sure his mother was home and on the mend.

"I'll make sure to let Mr. Gray know about the change. I hope everything turns out well."

"Thank you." He ended the call and pocketed the phone. He had to get this system finished.

When he returned, his father was awake. He gave him a rough hug. "How you doing, Dad?"

"Back is stiff from trying to sleep in that thing," he said, pointing to the chair, "but I'm fine."

"Justin, Jocelyn told me you were supposed to meet with a company today. Why did you cancel that appointment?"

Justin shot Jocelyn a look. "Mom, the meeting can wait. I needed to be sure you're okay."

She frowned. "Honey, you could have waited until after that meeting to come down here. Tell him, Jessie."

His dad raised his palms. "Now, Ruby, ain't no use in trying to keep these kids away. You knew they would be down here the moment I called." He placed a hand on Justin's shoulder. "This isn't going to ruin your chances with the company, is it?"

"No, sir. I just got off the phone and rescheduled the

appointment for next Friday. So don't worry. I've already made the slides for the presentation, as well as a demonstration of the system."

"I know you're going to do great," his mother said. "I'm so proud of you, all of you."

Justin sensed she was about to get emotional. "Mom, you should probably get some rest. You want to go home sooner, right? I'll take everybody to get some breakfast, and we'll be back in a little while."

"Oh, okay. I am a little tired." She yawned.

He and his sisters kissed her and stood back to wait for their father.

"I'm going to have Justin run me by the house to shower and change clothes. Don't you give these nurses any problems while I'm gone." His father placed a lingering kiss on his mother's lips, and the two shared a look of genuine adoration.

Although he was used to seeing his parents' expressions of love, this time Justin's thoughts went to Siobhan, shocking him and causing his heart rate to speed up. *Love*, as it pertained to him and a woman together, had never been used in the same sentence. *Love?* He sucked in a deep breath. He needed to slow down.

"Justin? What's wrong with you?"

His dad's voice broke into his thoughts. "Huh? What did you say, Dad?"

"What's the matter with you? You're standing there spacing out with this weird look on your face."

"Nothing. You ready?" His father studied Justin for a long moment then headed to the door. Jocelyn and Yvonne smiled at Justin, and he pointed to the door.

Instead of going to a restaurant, they went back to their parents' house, where Jocelyn and Yvonne prepared breakfast. Fatigue caught up with all of them, and instead of going back to the hospital right away, they decided to take a nap.

Justin woke up three hours later, and it took a second to remember where he was. He swung his legs over the side of the bed and sat for a few minutes to get his bearings. When his head cleared, he trekked to the kitchen for a glass of water. Not hearing anything, he assumed that no one else had awakened. He sat at the kitchen table and pulled out his phone to call Siobhan.

"Hey, baby," he said in response to her greeting.

"How's your mom?"

"She's okay. She's had the flu for a couple of weeks and now has an ear infection. She said she got light-headed before passing out. They're going to keep her for a day or two."

"I'm glad to hear it's not something more serious."

"Me, too."

"How long are you planning to stay?"

"I don't know. Through the weekend for sure, but probably early next week."

"Oh. That long."

"Yeah." He didn't know how he was going to take being away from Siobhan for a week. Lately, it had been hard getting through two days without seeing her. "How's your day going?" he asked to distract himself from the path his mind was heading down.

"Not too bad."

"Glad to hear it. Well, I'd better go. We're going back to the hospital. I'll call you later."

"Okay. I'll be thinking about you."

"I'll be thinking about you, too, sweetheart."

How was he going to tell her that he needed some space, some time to focus on his work without distractions?

"Well?" Cynthia asked when Siobhan hung up the phone.

Siobhan stared at her two friends across the table. "Justin's mom has the flu and an ear infection."

"I'm not asking about that. You two seem quite serious."

"I didn't plan for this to happen."

"Are you falling in love with him?" Kendra asked.

"I think so," she answered.

"Don't sound so sad about it, Siobhan. Falling in love is a beautiful thing. Just look at me and Cynthia or your parents."

"Yeah, but my judgment when it comes to men has been less than great." *Except for Justin.*

"Girl, that's a bunch of bull. You had *one* really bad relationship. Granted, it was a doozy, but it was only one. I wasn't going to say anything, but this has gone on for far too long."

"What do you mean, Kendra?"

"Malcolm, Arthur…and don't think we didn't know about that guy in college. Everybody's had something terrible happen or had their hearts broken, and they wallow in it for a while, then move on. But you've been punishing yourself for sixteen years for stuff that wasn't your fault, and you think by controlling everything around you and working hard enough, it will somehow atone for some crazy perceived mistake. The only problem is, you didn't mess up. You are not responsible for other people's choices."

"Exactly," Cynthia said. "And I know you're already trying to find some lame excuse to break up with Justin."

"No, I'm not," she argued.

"Mmm-hmm. Okay, so have you told him your real name?"

"No," Siobhan confessed on a ragged sigh. "I was going to."

Kendra pinned her with an angry stare. "When? When you're signing the marriage certificate and he just happens to glance over at your driver's license?"

"No. I'm going to tell him when he comes back." She hadn't planned to wait so long to disclose her identity. "Truthfully, I hadn't expected to be in the relationship long enough for it to matter. Can we please just drop this and eat?"

Cynthia's gaze softened. "We don't mean to upset you, but we haven't seen you so relaxed and happy in years. Being with Justin is good for you."

Siobhan couldn't deny that Justin brought out a side in her that she didn't often reveal. With him, she never had to worry about tempering her speech or being on guard waiting for him to ask about her family's business.

Somehow she forced down the rest of her soup, promised to call her friends and went back to her office.

While sitting, she closed her eyes and imagined what it would be like to come home to Justin every night—to see his sexy smile, to hear him say he loved her, to taste his tender kisses, to feel him sliding in and out of her as he made love to her. But life never worked out like that for her.

"Knock, knock."

Siobhan's eyes snapped open. "Come in."

Morgan entered with a sullen expression and dropped down in the nearest chair. "Can I talk to you for a minute?"

"Sure. What's wrong?"

"I don't think I can do this."

"Do what?"

"This case." She threw up her hands. "I've seen some of the pictures, and it doesn't look good."

"But you know things aren't always how they look sometimes. Morgan, it's only been a week."

"I know, but what if I lose? I don't know why Daddy gave this case to me," she grumbled. "There are two other lawyers who have years of experience, and he gives the hardest case in the company's history to somebody who's been out of law school two years."

"Obviously he believes you're the best one for the job. You're tenacious and confident, you don't back down and you have a big heart. Maybe it's the combination of all those things—being able to push hard when necessary, but also knowing when a soft touch is needed."

"I guess. But I don't like losing."

Siobhan chuckled. "Who says you're going to lose?"

"You haven't seen the reports and the pictures. They're going to be saying all these terrible things about us."

"Morgan, you can't worry about things you have no control over." As soon as the words were out of her mouth, Siobhan went still. She sat up abruptly and smiled tensely. "Hang in there, sis. You'll do fine. Dad did the same thing to Brandon and me. For some reason he has this baptism-by-fire thing going when it comes to us."

Morgan released a deep sigh. "At least I know now that I'm not the only one."

"Nope. Like I said before, you should think of this as your proving ground for when you get that first sports client. You're going to have to face down some tough old men."

"Please, that's no big deal. I *know* football."

She shook her head. "Ain't that the truth." Poor Malcolm had suffered with his sister's sideline coaching from the first time he picked up a football at age eight, and it continued to this day. He was probably the only NFL player with a private coach. "Speaking of football, is Malcolm back from Belize?"

"He'll be back Monday." Morgan stood. "Thanks for the pep talk. By the way, that's some good advice. You know... not worrying about things you can't control... Too bad you don't listen to yourself." She winked. "See you later."

Siobhan stared at the space Morgan had vacated. She was getting it from all sides today. Siobhan had tried to let go, but recalling her father teasingly saying before they left that day, *Make sure Malcolm doesn't try any of those daredevil tricks*, and seeing her parents' expressions after the accident, she couldn't help but blame herself. And dealing with the drama that came with her relationships... Didn't they understand life was so much easier when she set the rules and called the shots? Letting go meant opening up and possibly getting hurt, and with what she felt for Justin, this time would be worse. "I can't do this right now," she muttered.

She flipped open a file, and for the next few hours, she maintained a steady work flow and responded to several media questions from the contact log they had set up.

Hours later, she heard her cell chime, letting her know she'd missed a call. She groaned. *Please don't let this be somebody else wanting to tell me what to do.* She snatched it up and pressed the button without looking at the display.

"Hey, Siobhan. Still at the hospital and may not get home until late. Been thinking about us, and want to talk when I get back. Will try to call, but I have a big project to finish. Later, beautiful."

She'd been thinking about them and wanted to talk to him, too. He needed to know who she was. It would be up to him to decide whether to walk away.

Chapter 16

Justin shifted in his seat and adjusted the temperature. They had been on the road for three hours and still had a ways to go. "It is ten o'clock on a Tuesday night. Why are all these cars out?" His mother had come home on Friday, but Yvonne had to get back to work and left on Saturday. He'd stayed around to help his parents until he was sure his mother wouldn't relapse.

"Maybe they're all workaholics like you," Jocelyn joked.

"Ha-ha." As of late, he hadn't worked enough. "Are you going to be able to catch up on your lectures?"

"Yes. Alana took notes and emailed them to me already. I'm glad my first class isn't until noon tomorrow. Otherwise I'd fall flat on my face."

"You can stay at the house tonight if you want. Actually, I'd feel better if you did. I don't want you driving back to campus this late."

"I had planned to anyway. I don't feel like driving."

It took another hour to make it home. Jocelyn said goodnight and went straight to her room.

Justin took a quick shower and drove over to Siobhan's
house. He'd originally intended to go tomorrow, but he had
to talk to her tonight. He spent the entire ride rehearsing in
his mind what he would say. He still wanted to see her, but
needed a few weeks to complete his project. They could do
an occasional dinner and he'd call, but their time together
would be limited. A churning started in his stomach at
that thought. He had missed her like crazy this past week
and had contemplated at least twice driving back just to
spend a few hours with her.

The closer he got to her house, the more excited he became, and by the time he parked and walked up to her porch,
his body vibrated with sexual tension.

Justin took a couple of calming breaths and rang her
doorbell.

Siobhan heard her doorbell, glanced over at the clock and
frowned. It was almost midnight. Then her heart started
to pound, and her mind conjured up all kinds of bad sce-
narios. She jumped off the bed, grabbed her robe off the
chair and rushed toward the front. She flipped on the porch
light, saw Justin and hurriedly opened the door. She took his
hand. "Justin, come in. Is everything okay? Your mom…
Is she all right?"

Justin backed her into the house and shut the door. "She's
fine, but I'm not." He crushed her against him and inhaled
her startled gasp in a passionate kiss. He immediately tangled his tongue with hers, stripped off the robe, lifted her
in his arms and carried her over to the nearest piece of
furniture.

She felt the cool solid wood on her bare thighs, and it
took her a minute to realize it was the end table. He moved
between her legs and slid her panties to the side. His skilled
fingers parted her folds and stroked and teased her until
she was wet and trembling.

"Do you know how much I missed you?" he rasped out between kisses.

"I missed you, too." She unzipped his pants and he sprang, hot and thick, into her hands. Siobhan wrapped her hand around his hard shaft and whispered, "Show me how much you missed me."

That was all it took. "I hope you know what you're asking for." Justin nearly ripped her tank in half, and her breasts bounced free. The flimsy material hit the floor, followed by her shorts and panties.

He pushed her breasts together, captured her erect nipples between his lips and scraped his teeth gently over the sensitive peaks, and she cried out.

He took a condom out of his wallet and stepped out of his pants and briefs in one smooth action. Justin tossed the wallet on the floor, tore open the package and sheathed himself.

The wicked gleam in his eyes turned her on even more, and she whimpered. He nudged her thighs apart and drove deep, filling her completely and lifting her hips to meet his rapid thrusts. Sensations unlike anything Siobhan had ever experienced overtook her body, and she screamed his name. He spread her legs wider and hammered into her, demanding she give him everything. Her head thrashed back and forth, and she gripped the edge of the table as spasms of delight rocketed through her and she surrendered to a shuddering release.

Justin threw back his head and exploded with a harsh groan. "I missed you, baby."

Siobhan laughed tiredly. "I guess so."

"I'm not done yet. I have a week to make up for." He swept her into his arms and strode down the hall to her bedroom.

A few hours later, Justin silently rose from the bed and left Siobhan sleeping. So much for his little speech. The moment she had opened the door, all his good intentions flew right out the window. Seeing her tonight confirmed what his heart had been telling him—he was falling in love with her. He pulled on his pants and went out to his car to get his iPad. Working helped him think, and he had a lot to consider. He started to go back to the bedroom, but changed his mind because he would be too tempted to climb into bed with her. He stretched out on the sofa in the family room and opened his program. Now what? Siobhan had been adamant about not wanting a committed relationship and retreated every time he tried to get close. But he would give her time—he wanted her to fall right with him. Giving her up was not an option.

"Hey. What are you doing in here?"

Justin glanced up. "Hey. I didn't want to wake you." He set the iPad on the table and pulled her down onto his lap. He nuzzled her neck, inhaled her sweet, citrus fragrance and let the emotions he felt fill his heart.

"You said you wanted to talk when you came back."

"I did," he said slowly.

Siobhan angled her head to stare in his eyes. "What is it?"

"I want more than just a fling." He felt her stiffen and gently caressed her shoulders and arms. "Yes, I told you in the beginning that I wasn't looking for anything serious, and I wasn't. But my heart had other ideas. You are a remarkable woman, Siobhan, and I want only you."

"I don't know what to say."

He placed his hand on her heart. "Tell me what's here."

"I'm afraid of what I feel for you."

"Don't be, baby. You can trust in me." Seeing the tortured look on her face, he added, "Nothing's going to change, sweetheart. We'll just keep doing what we've been doing." He pressed a gentle kiss on her lips and just held her.

After a few minutes, Siobhan pointed to his iPad. "Were you playing a game?"

"No." Justin reached for the device. "It's a home alert system I'm working on."

She sat up. "Really? Do you plan to bring it to market on your own?"

"I hope to get the backing of a corporate investor with this one, but if not, I will." He showed her how the program worked.

"This is fantastic, and much better than anything I've seen. My father would love to talk to you."

"Your father?"

She left his lap and paced in front of him, wringing her hands.

"Siobhan?"

"Um… I need to tell you something, and I hope you won't be too angry with me."

He rose to his feet slowly. "What is it?" he asked with concern.

"I should have told you before, but… I wasn't… We weren't…"

He placed his hands on her shoulders. "Baby, just tell me."

Holding his gaze, she said, "My name is Siobhan *Gray*."

It took a moment, and then understanding dawned. He dropped his hands and took a step back. "All this time," he whispered in disbelief. Now he knew why she had looked familiar that first night. When researching the Grays, he'd seen a family picture. But in it, she was younger and her hair much longer, which was why he didn't recognize her.

"Justin, let me explain." She reclaimed the distance and reached for him.

He lifted his hands. "No. Why did you lie?" Justin was torn between wanting to hear her reasoning and leaving. His younger self would have stormed angrily out the door one second after she finished her sentence, but the older, and hopefully more mature, man in him demanded that he listen. Reining in his temper, he took a seat on the sofa and waited.

"I had already planned to tell you my real last name when you came back because I…I want more, too."

Her admission deflated some of Justin's fury.

"Every time a man finds out who I am, they see me as an easy way to get into the company."

"That night at the gala?"

She nodded. "Before you, there had been at least half a dozen men trying to hand me their business cards, promising me dinners and pitching their ideas. I thought you were after the same thing, so I used my mother's maiden name." Siobhan perched on the edge of the chair. "I was engaged two years ago."

His eyes widened. *Engaged?*

"Turns out he was another one only interested in money. He stole money from my bank account and had plans to get his hands on my company shares as soon as we were married."

Justin sat, stunned. He didn't know what to say.

"Justin, please know that I never meant to hurt you."

"I know. You were trying to protect yourself."

"So—"

"This doesn't change the way I feel, Siobhan. I'd be lying if I said I wasn't a little upset, but I understand."

"Thank you. I meant what I said about your alert system. My dad's been looking for something innovative, and I think this is it. I can get you on his calendar, if you want."

"No, no, that's okay. I can handle it." She had given him the perfect opportunity to tell her about his upcoming meeting, but he feared she would assume he'd been stringing her along all this time for the same reason as countless other men.

"Are you sure? I can probably get you in much sooner than if you schedule it yourself."

"I'm positive. I want the product to stand for itself without any special favors. Promise me you'll let me do this on my own."

Siobhan smiled. "I promise. I can definitely say you aren't after me because of my family."

Justin stood and pulled her to her feet. "No, I'm not. I fell for you *before* you told me who you were. Always remember that."

She leaned up and kissed him.

"I'm leaving so you can get a few hours of sleep. You're going to be exhausted."

She wrapped her arms around him. "You don't have to go."

"Yes, I do. It's almost four, and if I leave now, you can get about three hours in. I have the luxury of sleeping in, but you don't."

And he needed some time to figure out a way to tell her that the company had been his target all along.

Justin should have been tired after being up all night, but he hadn't been able to sleep after leaving Siobhan. And, with his brain racing as if it had a thousand open browsers, he hadn't been able to concentrate on work, either. He went back to the conversation he'd had with Bobby about the Gray family, and a lot of things made sense now. She was the PR director he had mentioned who kept people at a distance. What she had told him regarding her ex and other men in her past, plus the incident with her brother, explained her tough personality.

Another memory surfaced. The weekend they'd returned from Vegas, she had mentioned an emergency. Justin had been worried about her getting reprimanded, but he guessed being the boss, as well as the CEO's daughter, negated that possibility. Against his better judgment, he googled any recent incidents during that time frame and found out that someone was bringing a lawsuit against the company for a faulty product. He clicked on the link to a video press conference and turned up the sound. Bobby had been right; the woman knew how to handle her business. Her statement was simple, clear and gave only the facts, delivering the message in her usual confident way.

He rounded his desk and stretched out on the office sofa. Closing his eyes, Justin willed his mind blank. It worked for approximately five minutes. He let out a frustrated sigh. Why was it that the first time he was falling in love with a woman, things turned out to be so complicated?

Justin had asked Siobhan not to do anything on his behalf, and he sincerely prayed she wouldn't. If she decided to check the schedule or talk to her father's secretary, she would see his name. He didn't even want to imagine how upset she'd be.

"You're up early," Jocelyn said with a yawn, coming into the office and propping a hip on the arm of the sofa.

"Morning. Did you sleep well?"

"Yep. Judging by the fact that you're fully dressed at seven thirty in the morning, I'd say I'm the only one."

"Maybe I just decided to get up early."

She laughed. "First off, you've never been a morning person, and second, you smell like a woman. I recognize that fragrance."

"And?"

She raised her hands in mock surrender. "Hey, what you do is your business. It's just that there has never been a woman who's kept you up all night. Must mean she's pretty special."

"She is."

Jocelyn kissed Justin on the cheek and stood. "I'm happy for you. You want some breakfast before I leave?"

"Nah, but thanks. I'm going for a run in a bit. I'll fix something when I get back. What time are you leaving?"

"Around nine. By then a lot of the commuter traffic should be gone."

"I might not be back when you leave, so text me when you get to the campus."

She rolled her eyes. "You are such a big brother." She smiled and walked out.

No matter how old his sisters were, he would probably never stop worrying about them. Justin lay there awhile longer, then made slow steps to his room to change into his running gear. He really didn't feel like going today, but forced himself to get moving. With any luck, it would clear his mind enough so he could sleep.

After completing his run an hour later, it took great effort to get his weary body to his room and resist collapsing on the bed. He was hot, sweaty and in desperate need of a shower, but his muscles felt as heavy as lead. He managed to stay upright long enough to wash up, then slept for four solid hours.

Justin woke up well rested and with a much clearer head. His stomach growled, and he went to the kitchen to find something to eat. He found a note on the refrigerator from his sister.

I left you a plate in the microwave. You can thank me later ☺ Joce

He smiled, sent up a thank-you and reheated the pancakes and bacon.

With his stomach full and his mind and body renewed, he was able to make good progress in regulating the temperature feature. While it now maintained the room temperature, it still didn't register when a second one was introduced.

His cell rang, interrupting his flow. Justin activated the speaker without glancing at the display. "Hello."

"Hey, sexy. Did you get some rest?"

His head came up when he heard Siobhan's voice. "What's up, baby? I did sleep a little. What about you?"

"Somewhere around three hours. I'm tired, but in a good way."

"You don't plan on staying late today, do you?"

"Not too late. My brother Brandon has been camping out at my office making sure I leave at a decent hour," she added with a chuckle.

"I'm glad he's looking out for you."

"Of course you are...*men*. But it's okay when he does it. I bet you used to do the same thing."

"I plead the Fifth."

"What else would you say?"

He laughed. "I admit I did it a time or two when necessary."

"Uh-huh. I'm sure you called on necessity more times than not."

"So how's your day going?" Justin asked, changing the subject.

Siobhan burst out laughing. "Wow, real subtle. My day is fine. I was calling to see whether you were able to get on my dad's schedule."

His smile faded. "I spoke with his secretary, and I'll be meeting with him on Friday morning." He wasn't lying exactly because he had talked to the secretary, just not this morning.

"Great! That's a quick turnaround. Most times, it takes two or three weeks. He must have had a cancellation."

"Must have," he murmured. "Will you be there?"

"No. You'll be meeting with my dad, his partner Mr. Whitcomb and Brandon."

"What does your brother do?"

"He's in charge of the home-safety division for now, but will take over as CEO when my dad retires."

"Home-safety division? The company has more than one division?" Justin frowned, trying to recall if he'd read anything about another facet of the company.

"Technically, no, but my brother Khalil designed some fitness equipment for the disabled to put in his gym, and they thought it would be better to separate the two."

"Sounds like a wise decision. What are you going to be doing the rest of the week?"

"Tonight, I'm *sleeping*."

"Does that mean you don't want me to come over?"

"I'd love for you to come over, but we never get any sleep when you do. I have another press conference tomorrow, so I can't afford to fall asleep at the podium. But you can come by tomorrow night."

"Depending on how much I get done, I may have to take a rain check."

"I understand. But from what you showed me, it's going to be fantastic. Even Brandon will be impressed."

"I thought your father had the final decision."

"He does, but he relies on Brandon to keep up with the changes in technology."

One more thing to add to his growing list of concerns.

"Don't worry. I know my brother well and he's going to be all over this."

"You promised to—"

"I know, I know. I'm not going to mention anything. As far as they're concerned, I know nothing. What time is your meeting on Friday?"

"Ten. Why?"

"If you don't have any other meetings scheduled or will be otherwise occupied, I wanted to have lunch."

"I think that can be arranged."

"Just text me when you're done, and I'll meet you outside my father's office."

"Do you think that's a good idea? I mean, with what you told me about those other guys, I don't want him to think I'm after the same thing."

"He won't, and *I know* differently."

"All right."

"Well, I'd better get back to work. Call me later?"

"Definitely." They said their goodbyes, and he cut the connection. Justin pinched the bridge of his nose. She said she knew differently, and he hoped like hell it didn't change once she found out the truth.

Chapter 17

Friday morning, Justin arrived at the Gray Home Safety offices fifteen minutes early, filled with an unusual case of nervous tension. It had taken him the entire drive to realize the anxiety stemmed from his concerns about his and Siobhan's relationship and not the presentation.

"Mr. Cartwright?"

He stood at the secretary's approach. "Yes."

"They're ready for you. If you'll follow me, sir."

"Thank you." She escorted him through an outer office and into a small conference area where Mr. Gray and a younger man, who Justin assumed was Brandon Gray, were standing. Mr. Whitcomb sat in a wheelchair.

"Ah, good morning, Mr. Cartwright," Mr. Gray said. "I'm glad we've finally got our schedules together."

Justin shook the proffered hand. "So am I, sir."

"How's your mother? I hope it wasn't anything serious."

"She's fine, sir. Just a nasty bout of the flu. Thank you for asking."

Mr. Gray made the other introductions then said, "Let's get started."

Justin set up the projector and began. "In-home safety for the aging population has become an increasing concern. Many seniors are reluctant to move out of their own homes and want to maintain their privacy and dignity. This causes a high level of stress for both the parents and the caregivers. The SmartInHome Sensor System offers an easy way to keep elderly relatives in their homes as long as possible, even with memory issues." Justin detailed the different sensors for doors, keys, thermostat, kitchen appliances, bathroom and pillboxes. "Discreet sensors are placed around the home and send real-time data directly to your smartphone from a wireless hub."

"There are already a few of these systems on the market. I don't hear anything different about yours," Brandon interrupted, seemingly bored by the entire presentation. In contrast, both older men listened with rapt attention.

"There are two very distinct and critical differences in my system. One, while the others can only give you the room temperature, mine goes a step further and allows you to track body temperature, as well. And two, because the data is routed through the hub, there's no monthly subscription cost." He had even done a comparative cost analysis.

Brandon straightened in his seat. "Go on."

Justin smiled inwardly. "I can show you better than I can tell you." He had worked for twenty-four hours straight and finally got the temperatures to regulate. By Brandon's reaction, Justin was glad he'd solved the issue. He set up the demo, which had been calibrated for his body temperature, and placed sensors in the outer office. After instructing Brandon in its use, Justin went into the outer office, where he simulated several functions.

Upon his return, Mr. Whitcomb said, "I think I can speak for us all when I say this is one of the most innovative products I've seen in a long while." All three men wore huge grins.

"Now, I don't know what other companies you're negotiating with, but I'm sure we can come up with something to make it worth your while to join the Gray Home Safety family," Mr. Gray said.

Justin maintained his cool exterior demeanor, but inside he wanted to shout for joy. He listened as Brandon outlined some of the contract particulars. Justin clarified some key points regarding retaining design ownership. Although eager to partner, he didn't plan to hand over what he had worked so hard to build. Satisfied, he said, "I appreciate you taking time out of your busy schedule to see me."

Mr. Gray stood. "Thank you for coming. Could you wait a few moments while we discuss the compensation package?"

"Yes, sir." Ms. Avery appeared as if on cue and escorted Justin into a waiting area stocked with coffee, tea and a variety of snacks.

Thirty minutes later, they came back with an offer far above what Justin had expected.

"Would you be able to provide us with an answer by next Wednesday?" Mr. Gray asked.

"Yes, sir." He thanked them once again and took his leave. He didn't believe he would get a better offer, but had scheduled appointments with two other companies for the following Monday to explore all his options.

Out near the secretary's desk, he sent Siobhan a text. Less than two minutes later, she came toward him wearing a fitted black-and-tan blouse, a tan skirt that skimmed her curves and had a split in the front, and a pair of black pumps. It took everything in him not to throw her over his shoulder and find the nearest empty room. "Hey, baby." He gave her a brief kiss.

Siobhan smiled, and excitement shimmered in her eyes. "How did it go?"

"It went pretty well, I think. We can talk about it at lunch."

"I have a last-minute meeting in an hour, so it'll have to be quick. There's a café on the ground floor."

"Works for me." On the way out, Justin noticed Brandon had come out of his father's office and followed their departure with a narrowed gaze.

Over lunch he told Siobhan about the meeting.

"Did Brandon say anything?"

"He didn't seem too interested initially, until I mentioned the room and person temperature differentiation function and the no monthly cost."

"I knew that would get him," she said with a little laugh.

"I'll decide by next Wednesday. I want to weigh all my options."

"Of course. If you do accept, we'll have to go out and celebrate—my treat."

He had to tell her now. "Siobhan, I—"

"I have to go." She slid out of the booth and gave him a quick kiss. "I'll talk to you later."

He sighed inwardly. "Baby, I need to talk to you."

"We can talk later."

She opened her wallet, and he glared at her. "Weren't you leaving?"

"Fine." She pointed a finger his way. "But I'm paying for your celebration dinner." She spun on her heel and strode off.

As Justin had suspected, the offers from the other two companies didn't come close to the Grays'. Seeing no reason to wait, he called to accept the Grays' offer on Tuesday morning. He would go in on Friday morning to sign all the documents.

"Oh, my goodness! I'm so happy for you, baby," Siobhan said when he called to tell her the good news. "Do you want to go out tonight or tomorrow night?"

"Siobhan, you don't need to make a fuss. It's not that big of a deal."

"Are you kidding me? I don't know the details and I'm not asking, but the buzz going around has everyone here excited. So, yeah, it *is* a big deal. Let's try this again. Tonight or tomorrow?"

Justin really wanted to say neither, but he couldn't put off the conversation any longer. "Whatever is more convenient for you."

"Tonight, then. I know the perfect place. I'll make reservations and call you back."

It went against every grain of his manhood to allow a woman to pay, but he gritted his teeth and went along with her plans because it made her happy.

Siobhan hung up from Justin's phone call and did a little squeal. She was beyond excited for him and already envisioned some ideas for the marketing campaign. Turning to her computer, she googled the LA Prime restaurant in the Bonaventure Hotel, made a reservation for seven forty-five, then sent a text to Justin with the details. To save time, they agreed he would pick her up from the office at seven.

She was still smiling when Gordon marched into her office.

"What is all this?" he asked, waving a stack of papers.

"I have no idea. I haven't perfected the art of reading documents I can't see."

Gordon slammed the papers on her desk.

She peeked over. "Oh, I see you received my email."

"There is no reason to issue statements on all these... these internet sites," he said tersely. "We've always sent press releases to the news and radio stations and newspapers *only*, and there's never been a problem with the public getting our information."

Siobhan smiled sweetly. "Well, times and technology change, and we will change with them. You can either have those statements posted by noon as I asked, or you can explain to Brandon and my father why you think you're more qualified to make decisions about the company than they are."

Gordon visibly blanched. "Why wasn't I informed about this?"

"Last time I checked, you weren't a department head," she said mildly. "Is there anything else?"

He snatched up the papers and left in a huff.

She chuckled. Today, she wouldn't let anyone get under her skin. She had a man she was falling in love with, and they were celebrating the start of something great. Siobhan breezed through the rest of her day without incident. She laughed when she checked the company's Facebook and Twitter pages and saw her press releases. No doubt Gordon had to ask one of the younger technicians how to access them.

Leaving her desk, she made a trip to the bathroom to freshen up and reapply her makeup. By the time she returned, Justin had sent a text indicating he was in the lobby. No one had access to the upper floors without a badge after the offices had closed.

The moment she saw him, her pulse skipped. She threw her arms around him as soon as she was within reach and planted a kiss on him that left them both panting.

"Whoa, what a greeting," Justin said with a huge grin. "How was your day?"

"Better now that I'm in your arms."

He kissed her again. "Now, that's what a man likes to hear. Ready?"

Siobhan nodded.

"I'll bring you back to your car after dinner, then follow you home."

"I'm counting on it," she said with a sultry wink.

"You're about to get yourself in trouble. Keep talking like that, and I'm going to skip dinner and go straight for dessert. And you know how much I love dessert," he whispered close to her ear.

A shiver passed through her, and her nipples tightened beneath her blouse. "I think we'd better leave."

Justin laughed. "Hey, you started it. I'm just letting you know I'm willing and more than able to finish it."

She grabbed his hand and pulled him toward the parking garage.

He navigated the streets and made it to the hotel with ten minutes to spare. He left the car with the valet and escorted her up to the thirty-fifth floor, where they were seated near a window with a panoramic view of the city.

"How's your mom doing?" Siobhan asked.

"She's doing well. The ear infection is gone, and she's back to her old self."

"I'm glad to hear it."

"Me, too. Siobhan," Justin started.

"I already know what you're going to say. It's too expensive, and you don't want me to pay. We already had this conversation, and I'm not budging. You can pay for everything else from now on, but tonight, it's not happening, so relax and enjoy yourself. Didn't you tell me you had no problems sharing control?"

He opened his mouth, closed it again and shook his head. "That's not what I was talking about, and you know it."

"Mmm-hmm, but you said it and you weren't specific, so…" She let the sentence hang.

A slow smile started on his lips. "I see why you're the PR director."

Siobhan laughed and started humming the old Chaka Khan song "I'm Every Woman."

Justin joined in her laughter.

"So, have your feet touched the ground yet?"

"They never left. I'll admit that I think this will be a great product and do well in the market, but my main concern is the lives that will be saved because of it, and not so much the money."

Reason number twenty-five why I love this man. "What inspired you to do it?"

"When my grand—" He stopped midsentence and pulled out his cell. He frowned. "Can you excuse me just a minute? It's my dad."

"Of course. I hope everything is all right."

"Be back in a minute." He stood and walked to the front of the restaurant.

She opened the menu and studied the selections.

"Siobhan?"

Her head came up at the sound of an unfamiliar masculine voice. "Oh, hi, Bobby." Siobhan smiled. "It's been a long time. How's the wine business?"

Bobby leaned down and kissed her cheek. "It's good. I just flew in last night because I have a business dinner here. I see you and Justin connected."

"You know Justin?"

"We've been best friends since college. What do you think of his alert system?"

"It's fantastic, and I'm glad we'll be working together," she said warily. How did he know about the partnership? It hadn't been made public.

"I told him you were the best PR director in the business."

"You did? When?"

"At that safety banquet a few weeks back."

Dread uncoiled in Siobhan's belly. "You were there?"

"Yes, but I had to leave early." Bobby chuckled. "I guess Justin didn't need my help getting an introduction after all."

"Help?"

He nodded. "He had studied up on the best companies, and yours topped his list, so I got him an invitation to the fund-raiser. I'm glad he had a chance to talk to you guys."

The breath whooshed out of Siobhan as if she'd been sucker punched in the gut. It was all a lie. A fleeting memory crossed her mind of Justin saying she looked familiar. Had he known who she was the entire time? She glanced up to see Justin headed back to the table with a look of panic on his face. Tears filled her eyes. She shoved the chair back and came to her feet. "Can you excuse me, Bobby?"

"Ah, sure," he answered with confusion. "Is something wrong?"

"Ask your friend." She met Justin halfway, and he placed a hand on her arm to stop her. "Don't touch me," she gritted out and brushed past him.

Justin released her, held up his hands and followed. "Siobhan, please wait and let me explain."

She kept going until they had exited the restaurant. She turned back to him. "There's nothing left to explain. Bobby filled me in on everything."

"No, he didn't. Baby, it's not what you're thinking."

Ignoring him, she pulled out her phone and dialed her sister. "Morgan, I need you to pick me up at the Bonaventure. I'll tell you everything when you get here." She hung up without giving Morgan a chance to ask any questions. She jabbed the elevator button.

"Siobhan, please."

"No! You lied to me. All that talk at the gala about you just wanting to dance… It was all part of your game. I have to hand it to you," she said with a bitter chuckle. "You played the game better than anybody I've ever met."

"There was never any game," he said through clenched teeth.

"Really? So Bobby lied about you being there to meet someone from my family's company?"

"No, but—"

"That's what I thought," she said, stepping into the elevator. She should have known he was going to follow. Siobhan moved to the opposite side of the car and did her best to ignore him. Once again, she had been foolish. When would she ever learn?

"I did come to talk to your father, but I had no idea who you were. All I saw was a beautiful woman who captured my attention and held it tight."

"Nice try." The doors opened on the bottom floor, and she stalked across the lobby to the entrance with Justin on her heels. "Stop following me. You got what you want, so you don't need to pretend anymore." A few people paused to view the heated interchange. She never aired her dirty laundry in public, but tonight Siobhan didn't care.

"I'm not pretending, but what about you? You want to talk pretending? Fine. I'm not the one who lied about my identity," he snapped. "You are. So I'd be careful about pointing fingers."

"If you don't get away from me, I'm calling security."

Justin blew out a long breath, scrubbed a hand down his face and said quietly, "Look, Siobhan, I'm sorry. Sweetheart, no matter what you think, I did not betray your trust, and I'm not like those other guys."

She clenched her teeth to keep from crying. She would not let this man see her break down. "You're right. You're worse than they were." Siobhan was sorry, too—sorry that she'd danced with him, sorry that she'd agreed to go out with him and sorry that she'd given him her heart.

Chapter 18

Justin stood stunned at the angry words Siobhan hurled at him. It nearly killed him to know she didn't believe in him. He had to make her understand.

"Siobhan, I love you and would never do anything to hurt you. I asked you to remember that I told you how I felt about you before you revealed your identity. And I'm hoping that you feel the same way, even though you're angry right now."

Siobhan turned her back to him and wouldn't acknowledge him. Deciding to let it go for now—there were too many people milling around—he said, "I'll wait with you until your sister comes. I don't want you to be out here by yourself." Justin lengthened the gap between them and continued to observe Siobhan's stiff posture. He wanted nothing more than to gather her in his arms and assure her that his love for her was real, but instead he kept his distance.

Several minutes later, a Dodge Challenger like something out of the *Fast and Furious* movies roared to a stop in front of Siobhan. He took a step when she opened the door and caught a glimpse of a younger woman with long hair behind the wheel.

Siobhan stiffened when he moved close to her. She glanced over her shoulder at him. "Justin, don't," she pleaded.

He nodded, placed a kiss of regret on her lips, shut the door behind her and stepped back. Justin stuck his hands in his pockets and stared after the car as it sped away. Pain unlike anything he had ever endured ripped through his chest. He'd lost her.

"Justin, what the hell is going on? I was talking to Siobhan, and one minute she's smiling and the next she's in tears and running out of the restaurant."

He turned to his confused friend. "How much time do you have?"

Concern creased Bobby's eyebrows. "As much time as you need."

They went back inside to one of the bars, and as soon as the bartender placed their beers in front of them, Justin took a long drink. "When did you get back?"

"Last night. Okay, let's have it, Justin."

"I'm in love with Siobhan."

Bobby's mouth dropped open. "When? How?"

"We met the night of the gala, but I didn't recognize her because the website photo was an old one—she looked much younger, and her hair was straight and long. And she told me her name was Siobhan *Hunter*."

"I don't understand."

Justin brought Bobby up to speed on the relationship, from dancing at the banquet and laughing over coffee, to walking on the beach and taking a trip to Vegas. "Man, the way her face lit up when she found out about the show…" He shook his head. "She had me from that moment on. It wasn't until a week ago that she told me her real name. By that time, I already had an appointment."

"Why didn't you just tell her then?"

"I had planned to, until she told me about her ex stealing her money."

"Let me guess—the jerk only wanted her for the name."

"Bingo. I was in the middle of telling her tonight when my dad called."

"And I made it worse by telling her why you went to the banquet."

"That about sums it up," Justin said, taking another swig of his beer.

"Damn. I'm sorry. I had no idea."

"It's not your fault." Siobhan had to learn to trust him.

"It's not yours, either. You're not out to get her money or her name. You have your own money."

"She doesn't know that. She asked a few questions when I took her to my house, but I didn't say much. I didn't want money to be a factor…for either of us."

"I hear you. Are you going after her?"

"I don't know."

"What about the contract with Gray's?"

"I'm considering pulling out. I haven't signed anything yet." He shrugged. "I had offers from two other companies."

Bobby set his bottle down with a thud. "You can't be serious. Hold up, Justin. You need to really think about pulling out of this deal. I know those other companies didn't come close to matching the offer from Gray's, and as far as international exposure, you're not going to find a better opportunity to make your products a household name."

"I thought it all mattered," he said absently. "Being with the best company, gaining international exposure…but I don't care anymore." He only wanted Siobhan.

Bobby sighed in exasperation. "Man, you've worked

your entire life for this moment, and you're ready to throw it away for a woman?"

Justin looked directly at Bobby. "In a heartbeat."

He nodded. "All right. If that's what you want to do, I'll help you in any way. And if Siobhan means that much to you, you should go after her. You didn't get this far by giving up."

"You're exactly right." She had accused him of being like the other men in her past, or worse, but he intended to prove her wrong no matter how long it took. Starting tonight. He pushed the bottle away from him and stood. "I have to go."

They shared a rough hug, and Bobby laughed. "If you need me, you know where to find me. I'll keep that bottle of wine on ice."

"You do that."

Justin had the valet bring his car, and he drove off in the direction of Siobhan's house. He questioned his sanity the entire way, but knew he wouldn't rest until he found out if she was okay. Forty-five minutes later, he rang her bell. The same woman he'd seen in the car answered the door.

"May I help you?"

"I'm Justin Cart—"

"I know who you are, Justin, and Siobhan doesn't want to see you."

"I want to make sure she's all right."

"What do you care? Haven't you done enough?"

"Actually, I haven't done anything, and if your sister would give me five minutes to explain, she'd know it, too. Even a guilty man gets a trial before he's sentenced to death."

She stared at him curiously, and the corner of her mouth tilted in a slight smile. "Do you love my sister?" she asked boldly.

"With all my heart," he answered without hesitation.

She angled her head and surveyed him. "Give her some time, okay? Good night." She closed the door softly before he could say anything.

Not knowing what else to do, Justin climbed into his car and made the journey home. Lying in bed later, he realized he didn't have any other choice. He'd make the call first thing in the morning.

"Is he gone?" Siobhan asked, coming into the family room, where Morgan sat sprawled on the love seat.

"Yep. You knew he would come, didn't you?"

She nodded.

"I told him what you said about not wanting to see him, but it would be nice to know why."

She lowered herself into one of the armchairs. "I thought Justin was different, but it turns out he's not. Gray Home Safety was his target from the night we met. Bobby Mitchell was at the restaurant, and he went on and on about how he'd got Justin the invitation to the fund-raiser, how glad he was that Justin and I had connected because Justin had done some research…"

"But that doesn't mean anything."

"Yes, it does, Morgan. Can't you see his intentions from the beginning were to get his product to the market through our company?"

Morgan sat up. "True, but you told me that he thought your last name was Hunter, so he had no way of getting to Dad through you."

"He could have been lying just to string me along." Her doorbell rang again. "Please don't tell me he's back," she mumbled.

"Probably the brothers," Morgan said, going to answer the door.

Siobhan hopped up and rushed behind her. *"What? Why did you call them?"*

"Just in case we needed backup."

This was the last thing she needed. All three of her brothers filed past her into the house looking as if they were ready to kill someone.

Of course, Brandon spoke first. "Siobhan, you have one minute to tell me why we shouldn't track down Justin right now."

Morgan raised her hand and smiled. "Ooh, I can answer that."

All eyes turned Morgan's way. Siobhan glared at her.

"It's easy. He didn't do anything."

Siobhan threw up her hands. "Were you not listening to what I just told you? The man used me to get into this company, and you call that *nothing*?"

"Correction—you just *think* he did because you found out from someone else that he wanted to partner with us. Never once did you say Justin asked you for a favor. *And* you lied to him about your name." She turned to her brothers. "She gave him Mom's maiden name, so he didn't even know her last name until a week ago, right, Siobhan? Did he ask you to make an appointment with Dad or in any way solicit your help?"

"Dammit, Morgan! Cut the legalese and make your point," Khalil said.

"I'm trying to make my point, but I can't do it if you keep interrupting and don't let Vonnie answer the questions."

Brandon swung his gaze back to Siobhan. "So answer the question."

With all eyes on her, she said softly, "No."

"Ha! I told you," Morgan said.

"Malcolm, get your twin," Khalil said. To Siobhan, he said, "Sis, if Justin never asked for your help, what makes you think he was out to do the same thing as Arthur?"

Siobhan's shoulders slumped, and the tears she'd been

holding back spilled down her cheeks. She couldn't take them all being against her. "Why are you all making it sound like this is my fault? I didn't do anything wrong."

Brandon came over and embraced her. "Whoa. No one said you did anything wrong. What it sounds like to me is a big misunderstanding between you and Justin. I can't believe I'm saying this," he muttered, "but I met him, and he seems like a good guy. And I can tell you that Dad gave him a card the night of the banquet and asked him to set up an appointment, which got canceled twice before this last time—once on our end and once on Justin's."

His words gave her something to think about. No, Justin hadn't asked for her help. He had adamantly refused it and specifically requested that she not influence her father in any way because he had wanted the product to stand on its own.

Siobhan buried her face in Brandon's chest, and the tears came faster. What had she done?

"Thank you for seeing me on such short notice, Mr. Gray," Justin said, entering the office and reaching out to shake the man's hand. "Nice to see you again, Brandon."

"Same here."

"Have a seat," Mr. Gray said. "You said you had an urgent matter to discuss. Is this about the alert system?"

"Yes and no." He searched his mind for a good way to express what he had come to say, and in the end, he just stated it simply and truthfully. "I'm in love with your daughter Siobhan."

Mr. Gray's eyes widened, and his face registered shock. "Oh. I didn't realize she was dating someone seriously."

Brandon, on the other hand, leaned back in his chair and rested his elbow on the table, a look of amusement on his face.

"I met her the same night I met you, and we've been

dating ever since, except I didn't find out until recently she was your daughter, *after* I fell in love with her." Justin wanted to be clear that his feelings for Siobhan had nothing to do with her name.

"I'm a little confused as to how you wouldn't know who she was."

"She told me her last name was Hunter."

Mr. Gray chuckled. "Ah, my DeAnna's maiden name. But you still haven't told me what this has to do with our partnership."

He took a deep breath. "Last night, a friend of mine mentioned to her that I had been looking to do business with you from the first before I had a chance to tell her. She assumed I had been using her...like her ex."

"And did you? If so, then I may have to rethink this partnership."

Brandon sat up abruptly. "Dad, you can't be serious. Their relationship has nothing to do with business."

"Ah, but it does, son. Integrity far outweighs money."

Justin nodded. "I agree completely, sir, and that's why I'm here." His stomach constricted, and the words got stuck in his throat. "I did not betray Siobhan's trust as she believes I did. The only thing I'm guilty of is not telling her I already had an appointment with you after she revealed her identity. I don't want to hurt her any further, so I believe it would be in my best interest to withdraw from our agreement."

"Don't you want to take some time to reconsider this decision?" Brandon asked. "I'm sure we could work something out."

"I wish there was another way, but as your father stated, integrity outweighs money. My integrity and your sister mean more to me than any amount of money."

"Dad?"

Mr. Gray shrugged. "Sounds like you've made up your mind, Justin."

"I apologize for the inconvenience, but yes, I've made up my mind." The responses of father and son were polar opposites. Mr. Gray reminded Justin of his first boss, a true old-school businessman who'd mastered the perfect harmony between money and family. It was, ultimately, what he wanted, too.

Mr. Gray nodded and clasped his hands together on the desk. "I respect your honesty. We have an appointment on Friday at eleven to sign the contract, correct?"

"Yes, sir."

"Then you'll have until that time to decide. If you're not in my office by eleven o'clock sharp, the deal is off. Are we clear?"

"Very." He stood and extended his hand. "Thank you for your time."

Justin exited the office and almost bowled Siobhan over. He reached out to steady her. "Sorry."

"Justin. I guess you came to sign on the dotted line."

"Actually, I came to talk to your father about withdrawing from our partnership."

"Why would you do that?" Siobhan asked with surprise.

"Do you really have to ask?" He shook his head. "You don't get it, Siobhan, do you? None of this matters if I can't have you. I can always find another backer, but I'll never find another you. See you around."

Justin turned and walked off. Seeing her again magnified the pain spreading through his chest. His business he could do without, but he could not live without Siobhan.

Siobhan entered her father's office and stopped short. Her father and Brandon were engaged in a heated discussion. "What's going on?"

They both looked her way, but it was Brandon who answered. "We just lost the biggest deal in the history of this company, that's what."

Her father waved him off. "We haven't lost anything."

Brandon slammed his hand on the desk. "Dad, did you not hear what the man said? He's withdrawing from the deal. Do you realize that's potentially millions of dollars going somewhere else?"

She could barely breathe. *Millions?* Justin had given up all this money. "Why?" she choked out.

"He has some asinine belief that if he does this, it'll prove to you that he wasn't after your name or money," Brandon said.

"That's enough, Brandon," her father cut in. "Go back to your office and cool down. I need to talk to your sister."

Brandon stomped past her and slammed the door behind him, causing Siobhan to jump.

"Have a seat, honey."

Siobhan sat in one of the visitor chairs, and her father took the other one.

"You want to tell me what's going on?"

"Justin probably already told you."

"He told me his side. Now I want to hear yours."

She swiped at the tears, and her father reached in his pocket and wiped them with his handkerchief, just like he used to do when she was little. She started at the beginning and told him everything that had happened up to the previous night.

He folded his arms and angled his head thoughtfully. "Well, you both made some mistakes. You should've never deceived him in the first place, and he should have come clean."

"I know, but you don't understand, Daddy."

"I think I do. I want you to listen to me, and listen good. I know that Arthur fellow hurt you pretty badly, but it's more than that. Sweetheart, you've been holding on to that guilt over Malcolm's accident for too long. Let it go. No one holds you responsible for your brother's antics. You were just a child yourself. We accepted long ago that we just needed to make sure we kept up the medical insurance and let him be." He shook his head. "I'm so sorry, baby girl. Had I known it was this bad, I would've said something years ago." He grasped her hands. "Let it go. We're very proud of you, always have been. I love you, so much."

"I love you, Daddy." Despite her best efforts, Siobhan broke down and sobbed, releasing decades of hurts and years of trying to be worthy of their love, when she'd had it all along.

He wrapped her in his protective arms and whispered that everything would be all right. He held her until the last tear had dried. "Now, Justin is a good man. I haven't seen too many young men with his integrity. He listened to your reasoning for lying about your name, and you owe him the same courtesy. It's only fair, and we taught you five to always choose what's right."

Siobhan hugged her father again. "Thank you, Daddy."

"You can thank me by living your life. It's been a long day. Now go home and get some rest. I'm going down to your brother's office and see if I can pull him off the ceiling."

She laughed.

"That boy is too intense. If he doesn't calm down, he's going to have a heart attack."

"Good luck." She kissed him on the cheek, went to her office, locked up and went home.

Siobhan had a lot to think about, and getting Justin back topped her list.

Chapter 19

Siobhan read Brandon's text and rolled her eyes. She typed back: U do not need to stop by on ur way home. I'm fine. Just taking the day off. First Morgan had called, and now Brandon was sending her messages. True, she had never taken a day off, but after yesterday, she was emotionally and physically drained and needed some time to regroup. It felt good to still be in her pajamas at eleven. She had been able to sleep for a few hours, but realized she wouldn't truly rest until she had a chance to talk to Justin.

She picked up the phone to call him and then put it down again. What she had to say could only be done face-to-face, but she didn't have his address. Siobhan tapped the phone against her chin and tried to recall the directions to his house. An idea came to her, one she probably shouldn't even think about, but hey, she was desperate. She tapped the button on her phone.

"Gray Home Safety, this is Gloria Avery. How can I help you?"

"Hi, Ms. Avery. This is Siobhan. I'm off-site today and planned to stop by Mr. Cartwright's house to drop off some information. However, I left his address in my office. Would you mind looking it up for me?" Siobhan held her breath, praying the woman wouldn't ask any questions.

"Certainly, Siobhan. Hold on while I get it."

"Thank you," she said, exhaling. She jotted down the address Ms. Avery gave her, thanked the woman and promptly ended the call. Too bad getting up the nerve to see Justin wouldn't be as easy.

She started toward her bedroom to get dressed, and the doorbell rang. "Good grief." Must be either Khalil or Malcolm. Sometimes she wished she were an only child. "This is really getting old, guys," she said, opening the door.

"I beg your pardon."

Siobhan gasped in surprise. "Mom. Sorry—I thought you were Malcolm or Khalil. Come in." She closed the door and led her mother to the family room. "Do you want some coffee or tea?"

"No, baby. I came to see how you're doing. Your dad told me you had a rough day yesterday."

She should have known her father would tell his wife. They shared everything, and after thirty-six years of marriage, they still dated. "I'm okay."

Her mother patted the space on the sofa next to her. "Come and sit." When Siobhan sat, her mother said, "You're so much like me when I was younger it's frightening— always trying to shoulder everybody's burdens and thinking you have to do everything yourself." She smiled softly.

"I don't remember you being that way."

"Because your father helped me to see that, although I was capable, I didn't have to do it all. But I'm not going to lecture you anymore. Your dad most likely did enough for the both of us," she added with a chuckle. "I just wanted to see for myself how you're doing."

Siobhan hugged her mom. "I love you, Mom."

"I love you, too. So, what's going on with this nice young man I heard so much about? Any progress?"

She laughed. "I knew it. That's the real reason you came over here."

"Well?"

"I haven't talked to him. I was just about to get dressed and go over."

"Without calling?"

"Um...yes."

"That's my girl."

"Mom?"

"What? I don't advocate for women to chase after men, but since you've already got him, it won't hurt to remind him why he chose you in the first place." Her mother smoothed down her cropped salt-and-pepper layers.

Siobhan's mouth dropped. She had never seen this side of her mother.

"You don't stay happily married all these years without a little spice," she added with a wink.

"Daddy had no idea what he was getting himself into when he met you, huh?"

"Honey, he still doesn't."

This had to be the most enlightening conversation she'd ever had with her mother. She couldn't wait to tell Morgan. "The three of us are going to have to schedule a mother-daughter day soon."

Her mom rose gracefully to her feet. "Let me know when. I can work around yours and Morgan's schedules."

"Okay."

"Oh, and invite Justin to the family dinner on Sunday."

"I'm not sure we'll be able to straighten things out."

She smiled knowingly. "You will. Are you expecting someone?" her mom asked when the bell rang.

"No, but Morgan called and Brandon sent texts. My

guess is it's Khalil or Malcolm." As she'd suspected, Khalil stood on the porch wearing athletic pants and an Under Armour shirt. He had clearly come from the gym. "Good morning. I'm fine."

"Morning. Brandon called and asked me to check on you. Hey, Mom, I didn't expect to see you," he said when their mother appeared in the doorway. He kissed her cheek.

"Good morning, son. Kiss your sister and tell her you'll see her later. She has some business to attend to."

Khalil divided his gaze between their mother and Siobhan. He kissed his sister. "Um, okay. I guess I'll see you later."

Hooking her arm in his, her mother said to him, "Since you have all this time on your hands, you can take your mother out to lunch."

Siobhan stifled a laugh and gave him a little wave.

He waved back and called over his shoulder, "I guess I'm going to lunch with Mom."

"Have fun," Siobhan said.

Her mother smiled. "Oh, we will. I want to find out if he's any closer to settling down than the last time I asked."

This time Siobhan couldn't hold back her laughter, especially when she saw the look of horror on her brother's face. She closed the door. *I love my family.*

The short conversation with her mother had helped tremendously. It was time to reclaim her man.

Siobhan checked her makeup one last time in the rearview mirror and got out of the car. She scanned the front of Justin's house. In the light of day, it was even more elegant, from the neatly manicured lawn and various annuals that lined the edges, to the stone siding accents and solid wood double doors. Gathering her courage, she rang the bell. After what seemed like forever, she heard the locks disengage.

"Siobhan, hey."

She stared at him. He looked as if he hadn't slept in days. "May I come in?"

Justin stepped back and gestured for her to step inside. He closed the door and moved past her toward the family room. "Have a seat."

She expected him to say something, anything, but he just sat silently across from her. "I'm sorry for dropping by unexpectedly, but I didn't want to take a chance of you not answering my calls."

"I don't recall giving you my address."

Siobhan hesitated a beat. "I...um...got it from the files."

"You're resourceful, if nothing else."

"Only when it's important."

"And is it?"

He was determined to make this difficult. "I'm sorry, Justin, for everything, and I don't want you to give up your dreams."

"I don't believe this." Justin leaped to his feet. "Are you the company representative who's supposed to convince me not to opt out of an opportunity of a lifetime?" he tossed out bitterly.

"No! You worked hard to get where you are and deserve the deal, and no one sent me."

"Is that the only reason you're here?"

She shook her head. "I came to apologize for all the terrible things I said to you and to hear the truth."

He sat back down, braced his forearms on his knees and bowed his head. "You really want to know the truth?"

"Yes."

"I said you looked familiar that first night, but I honestly didn't recognize you from your photo on the website. It wasn't until you told me who you were that I put two and two together." He lifted his head. "It was your eyes that stayed in my memory." Justin got up and paced. "I opened my mouth to tell you I had scheduled a meeting with your father. Then you mentioned what happened with your ex and all those other guys. He'd already hurt you, and I was afraid you'd think the same of me."

Siobhan came to her feet. "I don't know what to say except I messed up. From the start, I expected you to be like the other men in my past, so I responded in kind." She reached up and cupped his face in her hand. "You are nothing like those men, Justin Cartwright. You are the absolute best thing that has ever happened to me. Can you forgive me?"

"That goes two ways."

She nodded. "Are you really going to cancel the contract? I mean, I know you'll be successful if you strike out on your own or go with another company."

Justin rested his hands on her hips. "In a perfect world, I'd have both the partnership with Gray's and you. But if I had to choose, you would win, hands down. Sweetheart, without you, my success means nothing."

"Then let me be part of your perfect world, Justin."

His eyes lit up. "Are you saying…?"

"I'm saying *I love you*, Justin, and I want to be with you."

He pulled her into a crushing embrace. "Baby, you don't know how much I wanted to hear you say that." He placed butterfly kisses all over her face, lips and neck. "I love you, Siobhan."

Siobhan closed her eyes and basked in the love he so freely gave. She now understood what her mom meant. In his arms, she didn't have to be strong or in control. "What do we do now?"

He lifted his head and smiled. "We enjoy the ride."

Her lips parted, but before she could utter a word, Justin seized her mouth in a kiss so blatantly erotic she felt as if she might drown. She arched into him, wanting to feel every inch of his hard body against hers.

With a husky groan, he deepened the kiss and devoured her mouth until they were both trembling. "Siobhan."

"I want to ride," she said, reaching on tiptoe to kiss him again and grasping the solid bulge that had been pressed into her moments ago.

Justin groaned again and grasped her wrist. "We still need to talk."

Siobhan moaned in protest.

His low rumble vibrated through her. "I promise we'll finish what we've started." He took her by the hand and led her to the sofa. Sitting next to her, he said, "I don't want us to have this kind of misunderstanding again, Siobhan. We need to make a pact to always be honest with each other."

"I agree. No more secrets. I had a long talk with my father yesterday, and I'm finally letting go of all the baggage I've been carrying."

"That's good. I know you're a strong woman and can handle whatever comes your way, but it's okay to let someone help you out every now and again."

Siobhan recalled her mother's words and chuckled.

"What?"

"My mom stopped by this morning and said something similar."

"And moms are never wrong."

"No, they aren't." She paused. "So, um, are we done talking?"

Justin shook his head and laughed. "We're done, baby."

"Ooh, goodie." She jumped up from the sofa and went to get her purse.

"What are you doing?"

She retrieved a bottle and waved it in the air. "I brought my own dessert this time."

He threw back his head and roared.

"First one to the bedroom gets to be on top," she said and took off down the hallway.

Justin entered the room seconds after Siobhan, a shocked

look on his face. "I think I'm going to like seeing this side of you, Ms. Gray."

"You ain't seen nothing yet, baby," she said confidently. Her mother said to remind him why he'd chosen her in the first place. She planned to do that and show him why she would be the only woman he'd ever need.

Justin strode down the hallway toward Nolan Gray's office at ten fifty Friday morning.

"Good morning, Mr. Cartwright," Ms. Avery said when he reached her desk.

"Good morning, Ms. Avery. I have an eleven o'clock appointment with Mr. Gray."

She gestured to a chair. "Have a seat, and I'll let him know you're here."

"Thank you." While waiting, he thought about his afternoon with Siobhan yesterday. The things they did with that bottle of honey, and the way she teased and tormented him had him contemplating buying some stock in the product. He grew hard all over again remembering the way she dragged her tongue across his chest, over his stomach and down to his...

"Mr. Gray will see you now."

The sound of the secretary's voice cut into his lustful musings. His eyes snapped open, and a rush of heat stung his cheeks.

"Are you all right, sir?" she asked with concern.

"Yes." He smiled tightly and willed his erection to go down. Justin took a couple of deep breaths, stood and quickly fastened his suit jacket.

She escorted him into the office. "Can I bring you some coffee?"

"No, thank you. I'm fine."

"Very good." She left and closed the door behind her.

"Ah, right on time," Mr. Gray said, standing and extending his hand.

"You don't look at all surprised to see me," Justin said.

"I'm not. Have a seat. All the documents are here and ready to be signed."

He hesitantly lowered himself into the chair, slightly taken aback by the man's bold statement.

"Do you have any questions before we begin?"

Justin wanted to ask whether Mr. Whitcomb or Brandon would be joining them today, but answered, "No."

"Excellent. Let's get started."

They went over every aspect of the twenty-seven-page document, from ownership, exclusivity and licensing, to fees and payments, presales and customer support.

"We'll need you to come into the office to work with our software team. You can set your own hours. Our marketing team will be available to help you, as well."

"Is there a particular person in Marketing who I'll be working with?"

A smile played around Mr. Gray's lips. "I have a feeling you'll have access to as many people in the department as you'd like."

In the end, Justin signed his name on a business contract that would keep him busy for the foreseeable future. He had worked hard over the past decade, and a deep sense of accomplishment washed over him. But nothing compared to the fulfillment he found in Siobhan's arms. Hopefully, he'd be lucky enough to negotiate the deal of a lifetime.

The older man stood, and Justin followed suit. "I think that covers everything. Is there anything else you need from me?"

A broad smile spread across Justin's mouth. "I'm glad you asked, sir. As a matter of fact, there is."

Fifteen minutes later, Justin emerged from the office richer, in more ways than one.

* * *

Later that evening, loud banging on his front door interrupted Justin's phone call to his parents. "Mom, Dad, let me call you back. Somebody's at my door."

"Okay, honey," his mother said. "Congratulations, again."

"We'll see you soon," his dad added.

"Thanks. I'll talk to you both later."

He disconnected and went out to the front, wondering who the hell was banging on his door as if they'd lost their minds. Justin snatched the door open and was prepared to give a set down to the person, but chuckled when he saw the three men standing there, all wearing scowls. "So, I'm assuming this is the part where you warn me about hurting your sister. Gentlemen, please come in." He escorted the trio to his family room. "You guys want a beer?"

"No," Brandon answered.

Justin smiled inwardly at their "big, bad brother" personas. It didn't faze him one bit. He'd been playing that role a long time and wasn't intimidated easily, though all three eclipsed his height by a few inches, with Brandon being the tallest.

"I've already met Brandon. You must be Khalil," he said to the one who resembled a professional bodybuilder.

Khalil nodded.

"And you must be Malcolm—daredevil extraordinaire and running back for the Los Angeles Cobras football team."

Malcolm smiled.

"Obviously you're here because your father let you in on my plans. Should I even ask how you got my address?" he said, looking directly at Brandon. "You all really need to do something about the lax security at your company. Now that we've got the introductions out of the way, you have questions and I have answers. So, fire away." Justin leaned back in his chair, folded his arms and smiled at their baffled expressions.

Malcolm said, "We just want to know if you truly love Siobhan. The last guy who claimed to love her ripped her heart out, and if it happens again, I'll rip *your* heart out."

Justin leaned forward and said with lethal calmness, "I know all about what that lowlife did to her, but I'm not him. Make no mistake, I will not allow *anybody* to hurt her again, including you." He let his gaze linger on each of them long enough for them to get his message. "Better yet, why don't you ask Brandon whether I love Siobhan. He knows *exactly* what I was willing to give up to have her."

A slow smile started on Khalil's face. "I think I'll take that beer now."

"Make that two," Brandon added.

Justin brought back beers for all of them. They laughed and told stories, and by the time the men left, he had a free membership to Khalil's fitness center and season tickets to the Cobras home football games. Not a bad haul for an interrogation.

There was only one thing he needed now.

Chapter 20

Siobhan opened the door to Justin on Sunday afternoon and greeted him with a passionate kiss. "Come on in. You're early. I thought you were going to be here around three thirty."

"I can't spend a little private time with my baby?" Justin asked, following her back to the family room and sitting next to her on the sofa. "I've been so busy these last couple of days that we haven't had a chance to talk."

"I know, but I understand. Daddy said you'd be coming into the office to work with the software-development team."

"Yep. I'll probably start with fifteen to twenty hours a week initially, then decrease as things progress."

"Maybe we can find you an office close to mine," she said, batting her eyes.

"No," he said firmly. "There is no way I'm having an office next to yours. I wouldn't get one ounce of work done. No way, not happening."

She scooted closer and let her lips brush his earlobe. He shivered in response. "Not even if I promise to give you the ride of your life?"

Justin hopped up from his seat. "This was a bad idea. If you keep talking like that, we aren't going to make it to your parents' on time."

Siobhan was eye level with the solid bulge pressing tightly against his trousers. She reached out and caressed him. "We don't have to be there for another hour. That's more than enough time for a quickie."

Before she finished her sentence, Justin had her on her feet and nearly sprinted down the hall to her bedroom.

They made it to her parents' house at four thirty-five. Her body was still humming, and she hoped her mother wouldn't try to keep them all night because that little interlude had only whetted her appetite.

"You know, it's not good to be late the first time I meet your parents."

"You already met my dad, so technically, it's just my mom."

"I met your father as a *business partner*, not as the man dating his daughter. There's a difference. And stop looking at me like that."

"I don't know what you mean," she said with a coy smile.

Justin got out of the car and came around to her side. "Behave yourself."

She laughed. "Hey, it's your fault. *You're* the one who said I need to let go."

He shook his head.

"Go ahead—admit it. You like it."

"Correction—I *love* it." He gave her a quick kiss. "Now come on. Making me late," he muttered.

Siobhan smiled. "I didn't hear you complaining thirty minutes ago." She passed her siblings' cars in the driveway and saw two unfamiliar ones parked in front of the house. "I wonder if my parents invited some other guests to dinner. I don't recognize those cars." She used her key to open the door and followed boisterous laughter to the back of the house.

"There you are," her mother said, rushing across the room. "We've been waiting for you two."

Siobhan kissed her mom's cheek. "We're only five minutes late. Mom, this is Justin Cartwright. Justin, my mom, DeAnna Gray."

"I'm so happy to finally meet you, Justin," she said, reaching out to hug him.

"It's a pleasure to meet you, too, Mrs. Gray," Justin said.

"Well, come on in and get comfortable. We have some friends visiting from out of town here, as well. Dinner will be ready shortly." She leaned over and whispered to Siobhan, "He's a good-looking young man."

"Thanks, Mom. Do you need some help in the kitchen?"

"No, baby. You go entertain Justin."

Siobhan made another round of introductions to her siblings. Morgan responded pleasantly, but Siobhan wanted to shoot her brothers. All three of them were barely cordial, reminding her of how they had behaved as teenagers. She was curious about the older couple conversing with her father and the two young women with them. Before she could ask, her mother called everyone to the table. Siobhan and Morgan helped bring out the food, and afterward, her father recited the blessing.

Lively conversation began again as dishes were passed around.

"Justin, I understand congratulations are in order," her mother said halfway through the meal.

"Thank you. I'm looking forward to working with the team."

"This is going to be great all around," her father added with a wide grin.

"Seems like that's not the only merger you're interested in," Brandon said mildly, not looking up from his plate.

Siobhan froze with her fork in her mouth. She pulled it out slowly and skewered her brother with a look. "Brandon, don't start," she warned.

Khalil shrugged. "Well, he is sitting at the *family* dinner, so maybe Brandon has a point."

"What is wrong with you two? Knock it off," she gritted out. She stole a glimpse at Justin, who continued eating as if her brothers hadn't said a word, and she wished she could do the same. But all she wanted to do was jump across the table and punch them.

"I guess he's not man enough to speak for himself since Siobhan seems to be doing all the talking for him," Malcolm chimed in.

Justin lifted his head and glanced at Malcolm, then Siobhan, squeezing her hand under the table.

"Dad, can you make them stop?" She was getting angry now.

"All right, boys. You're upsetting your sister, so lay off."

"Well, he hasn't said a word, so we're just wondering if he has anything to say for himself," Brandon said mildly.

"Yeah," Khalil said. "Do you have anything to say, Justin?"

"Actually," Justin said, shoving his chair back, tossing his napkin on the table and rising to his feet, "I have a lot to say."

The tone of his voice made Siobhan's heart leap in her throat. This would not end well. She pushed her chair back and started to stand. Then Justin lowered to one knee next to her. Her eyes darted around the table and met the smiling faces of everyone seated. His words held her spellbound.

"Siobhan, I grew up chasing what I thought were my dreams. But, since the night I met you, I've come to realize that you are, and have always been, my dream. I want your heart to feel and your soul to know that this deep love I have is yours, and yours alone. They say that the love of a good woman sets something free inside a man's heart. And that's what you've done for me. Your love is all I want, all I'll ever need, now and forever. Will you make me the happiest man alive and marry me?"

"You'd better believe I will," she said, smiling so hard her cheeks hurt. He pulled a small ring box from his pocket, revealed a heart-shaped diamond solitaire with a pear-shaped sapphire on either side and slid the ring on her finger. "It's absolutely *beautiful*. I love you."

"I love you, too, baby." He leaned up to kiss her, and the table erupted in cheers.

"Hallelujah, grandchildren!" Siobhan's mother cheered.

"Amen!" the other woman agreed.

Siobhan snapped her head around at the woman who, like her husband and two daughters, was smiling as if she knew something Siobhan didn't. She turned back to Justin.

He rose and pulled her to her feet. Draping an arm around her waist, he said, "Siobhan, I'd like you to meet my parents, Jessie and Ruby Cartwright, and my sisters, Yvonne and Jocelyn."

Her hands flew to her mouth. "Oh, my God! You planned all this?"

Justin smiled and nodded.

She glared at her brothers. "All that…that talk earlier was just an act?"

Khalil nodded. "We got to know Justin Friday night. He's a good man, sis."

They all nodded in agreement. Tears sprang to her eyes. Siobhan glanced around the table and met each of her family member's faces. "I love you guys so much." To Justin's family, she said, "I am so happy to meet you all, and I thank you for your wonderful son. He has enriched my life in ways I can't begin to explain, and…" She paused to gain control of her emotions. "And I want to assure you that I will always take good care of his heart."

Justin's family came around the table, expressed their delight and welcomed her to their family. Her relatives joined them, and another round of hugs, back slaps and handshakes ensued.

Finally, her father signaled for quiet. He waited until everyone settled down and reclaimed their seats. "I'd like to propose a toast to the newly engaged couple. First, I want to thank Jessie, Ruby, Yvonne and Jocelyn for coming to share in this milestone event. You have raised an outstanding young man, and it gives us great pleasure to welcome you all to our family. Siobhan, your mother and I have had the privilege and honor to be your parents for thirty-three years, and we are so proud of the woman you've become. With Justin at your side, and the love you two so obviously share, nothing will be impossible." He raised his glass. "May the love you share now endure and grow forevermore. To Justin and Siobhan."

Siobhan sipped from her glass and smiled over at her future husband. "Thank you for all this." Her emotions bubbled up once more. She put a hand on her chest and closed her eyes briefly. "And your family is here, too."

Justin took his napkin, gently dabbed at her tears and kissed her softly. "Sweetheart, you are my life and I'd give you the world if I could."

He kissed her again, and she forgot they were sitting at a table full of people until Malcolm's voice interrupted.

"Yo, man. She's still my sister."

Justin smiled. "She may be your sister, but she's going to be *my wife*, and that trumps your brother card all day, every day."

Everyone laughed, and Malcolm held up his hands in mock surrender. The remainder of the evening was filled with both families learning more about each other. Siobhan found Justin's family to be just as wonderful as their son and brother.

She had never been happier.

Justin and Siobhan sat cuddled in his oversize recliner late Sunday evening listening to music and talking about their whirlwind day. Seeing her interact with his family had filled his heart with joy.

"I can't believe you tricked me like that," Siobhan said. "And you got my brothers to go along with it, too."

"I like your brothers. They're good guys, and they love you. Khalil offered me a membership at his gym, and Malcolm's giving me season tickets to all his home games."

She angled her head. "*Really?* That's a first. The only thing they offered any of my other boyfriends was a threat."

He chuckled. "That's because none of them passed the test."

"And what test would that be?"

"Loving you," he said simply. He had never been concerned about her brothers because everything about his love for Siobhan was real. "So, when do you want to get married?"

"July of this year at the beach."

That was his baby—always ready with a frank answer. "Not that I'm complaining or anything, but isn't that a little soon? That's, like, only six weeks away."

"I know."

Justin pulled her closer and dropped a kiss on her forehead. "Whatever you want, sweetheart."

He'd told her earlier that he would give her the world if he could, and he meant every word. If she wanted a beach wedding, he'd make sure she had one beyond her wildest imagination. She was his heart, his dream and his greatest success.

Epilogue

Six weeks later

Siobhan locked her arm in her father's and made her way down the aisle to where Justin stood waiting. She had asked for a beach wedding, and he'd surpassed her deepest fantasies. A warm breeze blew across her face, the moon illuminated the clear night sky surrounded by a million stars, and torches provided light for her path and for the crowd of guests who had come to witness this special evening. She couldn't have asked for more.

"You take my breath away," Justin whispered when she reached him.

"And you, mine." They shared a smile and faced the minister. Twenty minutes later, she heard the words she had been waiting for since the day he proposed.

"I now pronounce you husband and wife. Justin, you may kiss your bride."

Justin touched his mouth to hers, intending for it to

be brief, but Siobhan had other ideas. She had waited her entire life for this man, and she wanted him to know the depths of her love. She wound her arms around his neck and took over the kiss, sliding her tongue between his lips and twining it with his. When she eventually ended the kiss, both were gasping for breath. "That ought to hold you until later," Siobhan whispered.

He shook his head. "You are something else."

After hundreds of photos, they entered the reception area under a hail of whistles and applause. She waved at her family. Her grandparents on both sides had come, and her mother's twin brothers, together with their families, had traveled from Sacramento. Siobhan glanced over at the head table where Kendra and Cynthia sat and shook her head. Those two hadn't stopped crying yet.

Later, Siobhan had an opportunity to meet Justin's maternal grandmother, and just like grandparents often did, the woman slipped some money into Siobhan's hand and said, "Here's a little something for you, baby." It wasn't until Siobhan was steps away that she opened her hand and saw the crisp one-hundred-dollar bill. She turned her surprised gaze back, and the woman smiled.

She caught Justin's gaze and met him halfway. "It's time for our first dance as husband and wife." They had chosen one of her favorite songs by Eric Benet, "Real Love," because she felt it described their love now and forever. Justin rested his forehead against hers, and they swayed to the slow love song, their smiles communicating the words of their hearts. When the song ended, someone brought a chair and placed it at the edge of the dance floor.

Justin led her to the chair. "Have a seat. And enjoy the show." He tossed her a bold wink and strolled off.

"What is this man up to now?" she mumbled. She followed his movements, and her confusion increased when her three brothers joined him on the dance floor.

They all shed their tuxedo jackets, donned fedoras and stood poised for whatever came next. The music started, and her hand flew to her mouth. She sat transfixed as her husband and brothers broke out in a choreographed dance step to Michael Jackson's "Smooth Criminal." They executed the moves flawlessly, that circular moonwalk included. She was up on her feet clapping and rocking to the beat. He danced his way over to her and dipped her in a flourish to finish the dance.

"This has been the best day *ever*!" she squealed. "Wow! That was so good. You guys ought to take this show on the road." She laughed. "You don't do anything by half, do you, Justin Cartwright?"

"Not when it comes to you, sweetheart."

She hugged him tightly and whispered, "How long do we have to stay here?"

"Hopefully not long because I can't wait to get you upstairs." They were staying overnight at the hotel adjacent to the beach and flying out in the morning for two weeks of fun and sun in Barbados.

"Me, either."

"I've got a bottle of honey in my bag," they said at the same time, then burst out laughing.

"No more condoms."

Justin stared into her eyes. "Seriously?"

She nodded. "I want babies and more than one, so we need to get started."

A look of tenderness swept over his face. "Nothing would make me happier." He leaned in and feathered kisses all over her face.

She could hardly believe she had finally found unconditional love and acceptance—control freak and all—with someone who would protect and cherish her. Someone with whom she could share her dreams and fears. She had found someone to share her life, and it had all started with one tender kiss.

Siobhan closed her eyes and smiled, anticipating the amazing life that awaited them.

* * * * *

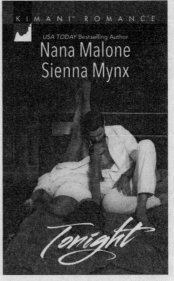